Who would want to shoot at her and Lee? Ellen wondered.

Probably the same people behind the other trouble the police department and her fellow K-9 officers had faced since being hired to solve Veronica Earnshaw's murder. Then again, Veronica's brother, Lee, had just been released from prison. *Could* it be someone after him?

The car was coming back. Lee pulled the two dog crates from the backseat of his truck and set them on the ground by the blown tire. Once he was sure they were out of the line of fire, he came to kneel next to her. "They're coming back."

She nodded, then raised her gun and aimed it. When the car crested the hill, she knew they were in for a second attack. "That's them."

The dark gray Buick slowed and the barrel of a rifle appeared in the window. She figured it was now or never and tightened her finger, heard the weapon bark, then felt the kick against her hand.

The sedan's front windshield exploded.

ROOKIE K-9 UNIT:
These lawmen solve the toughest cases
with the help of their brave canine partners

Lynette Eason is a bestselling, award-winning author who makes her home in South Carolina with her husband and two teenage children. She enjoys traveling, spending time with her family and teaching at various writing conferences around the country. She is a member of RWA (Romance Writers of America) and ACFW (American Christian Fiction Writers). Lynette can often be found online interacting with her readers. You can find her at facebook.com/lynette.eason and on Twitter, @lynetteeason.

Books by Lynette Eason

Love Inspired Suspense

Rookie K-9 Unit

Honor and Defend

Wrangler's Corner

The Lawman Returns
Rodeo Rescuer
Protecting Her Daughter

Capitol K-9 Unit

Trail of Evidence

Family Reunions

Hide and Seek
Christmas Cover-Up
Her Stolen Past

Rose Mountain Refuge

Agent Undercover
Holiday Hideout
Danger on the Mountain

Visit the Author Profile page at Harlequin.com for more titles.

HONOR AND DEFEND

LYNETTE EASON

HARLEQUIN® LOVE INSPIRED® SUSPENSE

Special thanks and acknowledgment are given to Lynette Eason for her contribution to the Rookie K-9 Unit miniseries.

Recycling programs for this product may not exist in your area.

LOVE INSPIRED BOOKS

ISBN-13: 978-0-373-44752-7

Honor and Defend

Copyright © 2016 by Harlequin Books S.A.

www.Harlequin.com

Printed in U.S.A.

"The LORD is good, a stronghold in the day of trouble;
and He knows those who trust in Him."
–*Nahum* 1:7

This book is dedicated to all of the heroes
in law enforcement—two-legged and four!
Thank you for your bravery, your service and most of all,
your dedication to justice. May the Lord bless you and
keep you, may the Lord make His face to shine upon you.

Acknowledgments

Thank you to my fellow authors for your tireless
willingness to answer my questions day and night!
Terri Reed, Lenora Worth, Dana Mentink, Valerie Hansen
and Shirlee McCoy. It's always a pleasure to work with
such professionals!

Thank you to Emily Rodmell for letting me do one more.
I appreciate you! :)

ONE

K-9 police officer Ellen Foxcroft shot a sideways glance at the man who drove in silent concentration. Just ten minutes ago, they'd picked up three puppies from Sophie Williams. Not only was Sophie a trainer for the Canyon County K-9 Training Center, she also worked with the Prison Pups program. A program Lee Earnshaw, the man behind the wheel, was intimately familiar with, since he'd been part of it up until two weeks ago when he'd been released from prison. Framed. Set up by a dirty cop, he'd lost two years of his life. He'd developed a new hardness and more lines around his eyes than when she'd last seen him.

Two of the dogs they'd just picked up from the prison program were ready to start training to be assistance animals for Ellen's clients—adults and children with disabilities. In addition to being a K-9 officer with the Desert Valley Police Department, she also ran the Desert Valley Canine Assistance program she'd started a few weeks before Lee was released. Already she and her four employees were making a difference in the lives of the people in their community, training the dogs to be service animals for the disabled.

Thanks to Sophie's generosity, Ellen hoped to have the two older puppies ready for the summer camp she planned to offer next month. The younger puppy needed more work—a job Lee would take on as soon as they got back to the facility. "You're awfully deep in thought," she said. "Are you all right?"

Lee blinked and sighed. "I'm fine. I just wish we had some better leads on who might have killed Veronica." Veronica Earnshaw, Lee's sister, had been murdered a little over three months ago. Her killer still walked the streets, and Ellen could tell Lee's frustration level was about to boil over.

"I know. We're working on it, Lee—we really are."

He scowled at her, then turned his attention back to the road. "That's what everyone says, I wish I could see evidence of that."

Ellen grimaced. She wished she could, too, frankly. "An investigation like this takes time. It's unfortunate, but it just does. At least you're out of prison now, and that happened as a result of this investigation. Look at the positive side."

His lips quirked. "You would look at it that way." The puppies in the travel carriers in the back barked and yipped. "I appreciate your giving me this chance to work with you and the pups. Not everyone believes I'm innocent, in spite of the press conference and Ken Bucks's arrest."

"You're welcome."

Former Desert Valley sheriff's deputy, Ken Bucks had been arrested and, in order to secure a deal and a lighter sentence for himself, had confessed to framing Lee and sending him to prison two years ago for a robbery he didn't commit. "I just really want to put it all behind me."

"I'm sure you do." Probably easier said than done. This was Lee's second day on the job. Two days ago, after much self-examination and encouragement from Sophie, she'd approached Lee about working for her, and he'd been reluctant. With their history, she couldn't say she blamed him. They'd dated in high school. Until she'd allowed her mother to chase him away. Her jaw tightened. She didn't want to go there.

Instead, she remembered the flare of attraction she'd felt just from being in his presence again. Just from talking to him and looking into his eyes. Eyes she'd never been able to forget.

Eyes that looked years older and much harder than she remembered. But she'd shoved aside her attraction— and her pride. After some fancy talking, he'd agreed to give working with her a trial run. She figured his love of animals and training had convinced him. She didn't care what it was, she was just glad he'd conceded. He'd started yesterday with a tour of Ellen's assistance facility, which connected to the Canyon County K-9 Training Center. "You know, I was thrilled when Veronica said she was fine with me leasing the unused portion of the K-9 training center."

"Veronica never was one to turn down money."

"Well, whatever her reasons, I'm just glad she let me."

Coming from a wealthy background, Ellen knew people looked at her differently, had various expectations of her, some good, some bad, most wrong. But at least she'd done something good with some of that wealth.

She'd started the program with money from her trust fund. And then listened when Sophie Williams insisted that Lee Earnshaw would be the perfect person to hire to help train the dogs.

Today she could see his eagerness to get started working with the new animals. "Sophie said when it came to working with the dogs at the Prison Pups program, you were the best she'd ever seen. She called you a dog whisperer." After Veronica had been killed, Sophie had taken over the program that trained dogs and rookie K-9 officers. She often used inmates at the prison to help with the training of the puppies until they were old enough for the center. Lee had been one of those inmates.

He gave a low laugh then frowned. "A dog whisperer?" He shrugged. "You know me. I've worked with animals all my life. I like them and they like me. The Prison Pups program was the only thing that kept me sane these past two years."

"I know. And I'm sorry."

"Yeah. I am, too, but it is what it is. I'm trying to move on."

"You're not bitter?"

He glanced at her from the corner of his eye. "I'm bitter. I just fight it on a daily basis, hoping I'll eventually win the battle."

"You will," she said. "Whatever happened to your plans to become a vet?"

He sighed and shrugged. "Life happened."

"But you graduated from college."

"Yes, with a degree in biology. I even started on graduate school, then everything kind of went south with Dad and I had to help him pay bills. Breeding and training dogs was the way to do that."

"Do you have plans to finish school?"

"Yes. One day. Ken Bucks kind of messed that up pretty good. And then Veronica was murdered..."

Ellen heard the unspoken end of the sentence—*and her killer is still out there.*

She couldn't help studying his features. Brown hair with a brand-new cut, brown eyes that at times looked hard and cold but were always alive and warm when he worked with the animals His strong jaw held a five-o'clock shadow. She used to kiss that jaw on a regular basis. She cleared her throat and tried to shake her memories, but they just wouldn't leave her alone. Memories of being his girlfriend, the vicious conflict with her mother. And then Lee had walked away from it all.

Now she was back in town and he was out of prison and she was working in Desert Valley. For the time being. Thanks to her mother's stipulation that she and the other rookies had to stay in Desert Valley until Veronica's murder was solved or she would withdraw the funding she'd given the department. Funding the department couldn't afford to lose. Ellen planned to have a few words about that with her mother when she woke from the coma she'd been in for the past three months. Someone had broken in to her home and attacked her, almost killing her. "I can understand your frustrations, Lee. I feel the same way about my mother's attacker." Ellen desperately wanted to find out who did it.

"I know, it's just—"

The back windshield shattered and Ellen gave a low scream of surprise. Lee jerked the wheel to the right. "Get down!" Outside sounds rushed through the missing window. Someone was shooting at them!

Ellen ignored his order and turned in her seat to look out the back. "He's coming up on your five o'clock. Coming in for another shot." It was the perfect place for an ambush. On a back road that didn't see much traffic just outside a small town.

Ellen's tension mounted and she was extremely glad she'd left Carly, her golden retriever K-9 partner, at the training center for this trip. It was supposed to take no more than two hours all in. An hour to the prison and an hour back. And while Lee had been as tense as she'd ever seen him at returning to the prison, he hadn't said a word. She released her weapon from its holster and gripped it in her right hand, readying herself for the next attack.

Four months, she thought.

Less than four months ago, she'd finished the twelve-week training session at the Canyon County K-9 Training Center. The state of Arizona had started the program years ago and found it quite successful. They trained new police academy recruits to be K-9 officers. She was a newbie, a rookie officer with the Desert Valley Police Department.

And now she might have to shoot someone.

The thought wanted to paralyze her, but her training kicked in and she knew she could do what she had to in order to protect herself and Lee.

The car roared up beside them and she got a brief glance at the driver and the gun he had pointed at her. Lee stomped the brakes, throwing her against the seat belt. She jerked forward then back, her head slamming into the headrest, her hand against the door. She lost her grip on the weapon and it clattered to the floor. The next shot took off the passenger-side mirror of the truck. Another hit a tire. Lee fought with the wheel and the truck listed to the side, but that didn't stop him.

He spun the wheel to the right and they roared onto a side road. The other vehicle swept past. Lee hit the brakes again and backed up, the truck lurching, the rim of the flattened tire grinding. But he managed to complete his three-point turn so that the front of his truck now faced the road. She watched the disappearing taillights of the other car.

As soon as Lee put the truck in Park, Ellen rolled out of the passenger door, grabbed her weapon from the floor and aimed in the direction the other car had gone. "Lee, are you okay? Come out the passenger door."

"I'm fine." He landed on the ground beside her, kneeling behind the protection of the open door. He radiated tension. "I'm going to check on the dogs."

Ellen registered the barking. "I'm calling for backup." She grabbed the radio from her hip and put in the call. When Dispatch answered, she rattled off the information. She glanced at Lee who was also watching the road. "Anything?"

"No, not yet."

"Help is on the way."

She maintained her vigilance even as her mind searched for answers. Who would want to attack her and Lee? Probably the same people behind the other trouble the police department and her fellow K-9 officers had faced since being assigned to solve Veronica Earnshaw's murder. Then again, Lee had just been released from prison. Could it be someone after him?

The drone of an engine caught her attention and all speculation fled. She heard it coming closer as Lee pulled the two crates from the backseat of the king cab one after the other and set them on the ground by the blown tire. He handled the heavy cargo as though it weighed nothing, but she knew the two six-month-old pups weighed about fifty pounds each. "I hear something. Are they coming back?"

"Sounds like it." She raised her gun and aimed it. When the car crested the hill, she knew they were in for a second attack. "That's them." The dark gray Buick slowed; the barrel of a rifle appeared in the window. She figured it was now or never and tightened her finger, heard her weapon bark, felt the kick against her hand.

The sedan's front windshield exploded. The driver hit the gas and the vehicle blew past in a drunken weave. Ellen spun from her position and moved to the back of the truck near the crated, yapping puppies. This time the car didn't turn around—and she got a partial plate. "Oh-four," she whispered. "I didn't get the rest of it. But I got 04."

She turned to find Lee hovering over the puppies, his features tense, face pale. "Are you all right?" he asked.

"Yeah. You?"

He nodded. "The puppies are fine, too."

Ellen pulled her phone from the clip on her belt. "I'm going to find out where backup is. Keep an eye out for them to come back while I'm on the phone, will you?" Not only did they need a tow truck for Lee's vehicle, they needed a ride back to town and a Be On the Lookout—a BOLO—put out for the gray sedan.

"Of course." He looked distracted. Thoughtful. His brows pulled together over the bridge of his nose as if he knew something and was pondering it.

"What is it?" she asked.

His eyes flicked to hers then he shook his head. "Nothing."

The dispatcher came on the line. "Where's my backup?"

"On the way, Ellen. They should be there within minutes."

"Tell them to be looking for a dark gray sedan—a Buick—with 04 in the license plate."

"Copy that."

Ellen hung up and paced behind the protection of Lee's truck while she watched the road and thought about what had just happened. "Did you tell anyone about us going to pick up the puppies?" she asked.

Lee frowned. "No. But it's not because I thought it was some top secret mission—it's just that I don't talk to too many people."

Ellen heard the bitterness behind the words. Being imprisoned for two years for a crime one didn't commit could do that to a person. She also knew that people in Desert Valley, Arizona, had long memories and weren't very forgiving. Never mind that the man before her had been set up by a corrupt cop.

When she'd heard Lee had been arrested for robbery, she'd been stunned. Then disbelief had set in. But the evidence had been overwhelming. Now she knew why. It was easy to frame someone when the investigating officer planted evidence. Disgust curled inside her. She had nothing but contempt for those who used their power to hurt others, to fulfill some kind of personal agenda.

Sirens broke the silence and she straightened, her eyes once again going to the place where the gray sedan had disappeared. Some of her adrenaline eased now that she felt sure they weren't coming back.

Chief of police Earl Jones stepped from his cruiser. Seventy years old, he topped six feet two inches and carried himself well in spite of his large gut. His gray hair looked mussed, as though he'd run his hands through it several times. His gaze landed on Ellen then slid over to Lee. "Not out of prison two weeks and you're already causing trouble? Not a good way to start your new life."

Lee nearly bit through his tongue to keep the words he'd like to fling at the man from making their way past his teeth. He simply stared at the chief. He wouldn't defend himself. He didn't have to. The fact that he stood here a free man was defense enough as far as he was concerned. Chief Jones raised a brow, a glint of respect lighting his eyes before he hitched his britches and held out a hand to Lee. "You got a raw deal. I'm glad it all worked out for you."

Lee blinked and swallowed his anger. He shook the man's hand. "Thanks. I am, too."

The chief looked at Ellen. "What's going on here, Foxcroft?"

Ellen's gaze darted between the two them. Lee maintained his cool stance. Deputy Louise Donaldson exited her cruiser and joined them on the side of the road. The woman was in her early sixties and, if Lee remembered correctly, had been widowed at a rather young age.

She was tall and solid, her hair cut in a no-nonsense brown bob. Her dark eyes were serious and concerned. He also knew she planned to retire soon. In fact he wondered who would retire first, the chief or Louise. And why he was even thinking about that confused him. He attributed it to some kind of coping mechanism. If he thought about the mundane, he didn't have to think about the fact that he and Ellen could have been killed a short few moments ago.

"We were shot at," Ellen was saying. "I think there were two of them in the vehicle. They drove a dark gray Buick and I got a partial plate." She gave it to him. "They've also got a busted windshield."

"I'll call for a tow truck," Louise said. She got on her phone and Earl rubbed a hand over his craggy face.

"All right, let's get you two back to town and get this figured out. Donaldson!"

"Yes, Chief?" She slid her phone back into the clip.

"Get Marlton and Harmon out here to take care of the evidence collection before the sun goes down. We've only got a couple hours before dark." Dennis Marlton and Eddie Harmon, two more of Desert Valley's finest— only Lee had come to figure out they weren't quite so fine. Between ready-for-retirement cops and simple ineffectiveness, Lee decided it was a wonder enforcement of the law even happened in Desert Valley.

Chief Jones was a good man, but his upcoming retirement had him slacking off. The chief continued, "I'll stay here while you chauffeur these two back to town. Officer Foxcroft's got some paperwork to fill out on the shooting. Make sure her gun is turned in and all is done according to procedure."

Louise's jaw tightened as though she didn't like being told how to do her job, but she simply nodded. "Of course. Come on."

Lee put the crated puppies in the back of the DVPD SUV cruiser then he climbed in the back while Ellen took the front passenger seat. Louise started the vehicle and pulled away from the edge of the road. Lee reached over and settled his hand on Ellen's shoulder. She started and turned to look at him, confusion clouding her eyes. But at least she didn't pull away. "I'm glad you're all right," he said. "That was some quick thinking and good shooting out there."

She shot him a tight smile. "Thanks. I just wanted to stop them."

"You did that, all right."

She fell silent and Lee removed his hand from her shoulder to look out the window and watch the scenery pass by. He didn't take for granted the fact that he could do this now. He'd missed riding in a car for the past two years. Missed driving his truck. He'd missed a lot of things. The anger wanted to bubble up, but he took a deep breath and forced it down. Anger at what he couldn't change wouldn't help anything. It would just cause the bitterness to grow, and he didn't want to go through life that way. Had made a vow he wouldn't let it consume him. Not like it had his father. He forced the thought away.

Within minutes they were at the police station. Lee climbed out of the cruiser, grabbed the puppies from the back and waited for Ellen to climb out. He let her go in front of him, watching her enter the station, her steps light, movements graceful. He realized his feelings for her hadn't diminished one bit from their high school days. No matter how hard he tried to deny it, he was still attracted to her. And her mother still hated him. No doubt even more so at this point. He wasn't just a kid from the wrong side of the tracks anymore—he'd been incarcerated. Oh, yes, that would go over well with Marian Foxcroft. Assuming she ever woke up from her coma to find out he was now out and working with her daughter. As much as he disliked the woman, he realized he could feel compassion for her. She was in the hospital in a coma, a victim of a home invasion and a vicious attack. No one deserved that. He swallowed hard and pulled the rolling crates behind him. He trailed Ellen as she led the way through the Desert Valley Police Department lobby.

"Ellen?"

Ellen paused and turned to the woman who'd called her name. "Yes, Carrie?"

Lee racked his brain trying to place what he'd learned about the secretary and couldn't come up with much. In her thirties, she wore thick horn-rimmed glasses and her brown hair was always in the same style every time he'd seen her around town. Up in one of those messy-bun things some women managed to twist their hair into. She was quiet and kind and did her job well if the rumors were true.

She handed Ellen a piece of paper. "The hospital called just to say there's been no change in your mother. Dr. North said to let you know he had a family emergency and wouldn't be able to meet with you this afternoon, but if you'll call his secretary to reschedule, she'll fit you in as soon as possible."

"That's fine. Thanks." She frowned. "I wonder why he didn't call my cell."

"He said he did but you didn't answer."

"She was kind of busy," Lee said.

Ellen nodded. "Thanks, Carrie."

"Of course." She turned back to her computer and Louise continued the trek to a conference room.

Officer Donaldson shut the door behind them and Lee saw Ellen check her phone. "Yep. Missed call." She glanced at Lee. "Right in the middle of our little incident. I never heard it ring."

He hadn't, either.

Ellen removed her weapon and placed it in the bag the officer held out for her. "You know the drill," Officer Donaldson said. "There'll be an investigation. You're off duty for the moment."

Ellen sighed. "I know."

"The good news is since there are no wounded or dead bodies, you could be cleared for return to duty as early as tomorrow or the next day. We'll let you know."

"Thanks, Louise."

The woman's brown eyes softened a fraction. "You're welcome. You did good, rookie."

Ellen gave a faint smile. "Thanks."

"How's your mother?"

Her smile slipped. "She's still alive. We're just praying she wakes up soon and can tell us who did this to her. Until then, she's under twenty-four-hour guard to make sure no one can get to her and finish what they started. Chief Jones was willing to have you all take shifts guarding her, but I know Mom wouldn't have wanted to take you away from your duties here. I've hired a private agency to make sure there's a guard on her door. So far, that's worked out well."

"We're all praying for her." Louise set the weapon aside and motioned for them to sit at the table. Once seated Lee wanted to fidget. He wasn't interested in being in this building ever again. Louise pulled a laptop in front of her. "All right, let's go through it all again."

Lee started to say something when Carrie entered the room. Louise raised a brow. "Yes?"

"Sorry to interrupt, but someone found a glove behind a Dumpster near veterinarian Tanya Fowler's office and brought it in." She held up the bagged glove while he pictured Tanya, the veterinarian he'd seen occasionally when she'd come to the prison to vaccinate the dogs with the Prison Pups program. A sweet lady whose nonjudgmental eyes never failed to raise his spirits. He tuned back into what Carrie was saying. "Two kids were waiting with their mother while she had their dog in with Dr. Fowler and they ran around the side of the building playing hide and seek. Little Justin Daniels found it and gave it to his mother."

"Okay. And it's important because…?"

"It matches the set worn by one of the robbers who robbed that bank in Flagstaff six months ago."

Louise frowned. "How would she have known that?"

"She wouldn't. She turned it in to us because it had five one-hundred-dollar bills in it and thought someone may have reported it missing."

"Has someone?"

"No." Carrie pushed her glasses up on the bridge of her nose with her forefinger. "But when the robbery first happened, we got all those wanted notices faxed to us, remember? The chief also got the video footage of the robbery." She walked farther into the room and placed the glove on the desk. "He and I watched it together just in case I spotted anyone hanging around town. Turns out I recognized the gloves in the surveillance video. They're a pretty popular brand and I sent this exact pair to a cousin for Christmas last year." She wrinkled her nose. "Well, not *this* one, but a pair just like them. So I just checked the bank footage again to be sure, and this sure looks like one of the gloves."

Louise nodded. "Okay, that's good news. I wouldn't have thought there would be any chance of picking up that trail again. Send the glove off to the lab. Take Justin Daniels's fingerprints as well as his mother's and send them for comparison." Carrie nodded. "Also, get the serial numbers from the bills and send them to the

Flagstaff PD. I don't know that they'll need them, but it can't hurt to have them just in case."

"Got it." Carrie turned and walked out, carrying the evidence.

Louise looked up at Ellen. "You heard about that bank robbery, right?"

"Vaguely. It happened shortly after we started our training with Veronica and that's where my focus was. I think I remember that they never found the money, right?"

"No, it happened just as the bank was closing on a Friday afternoon. Two men in masks and semiautomatics in broad daylight. Shook the whole city up."

"They were obviously professionals and they had it well planned."

"True," she sighed. "They got away that day, but the FBI was called in and arrested one of the robbers—a Nolan Little. The second robber got away, but the FBI tracked him down right here in Desert Valley two days later, hiding in an abandoned mobile home. He got into a shootout with them and was killed. They searched and found his weapon and a few bills, but he didn't have the bank money on him."

"Let me guess, the one they caught isn't talking."

"He couldn't if he wanted to. He was killed about two months into serving his sentence."

"So anyone who might have known where the money is can't talk because they're dead."

"Yes. At least the ones we know about."

"You think there's someone else involved?"

"The FBI was convinced there was a third person— a driver—but they've never been able to prove it. He wasn't in the video and there wasn't a car at the scene."

"How did they get away?" Ellen asked.

"On foot. Ran right out the back door through a back alley and disappeared. That's why we think there was a third person involved. Someone with a car that was never seen. Someone who knew where the security cameras were and made sure to park out of view. The robbers climbed in and they drove away." She sighed. "The FBI sends the chief an update every so often, but I think they've probably given up on ever recovering the money—or the third person if there ever was one." She shrugged. "Who knows? Maybe with the glove, they'll get a fresh trail to follow." She drew in a deep breath. "Now, Lee, what can you tell me about the shootout that just occurred?"

Lee shifted. "I think I have something that will help."

"What's that?"

"I have a dash cam on my truck. We just need to watch the video." He held up his phone and pressed the screen to pull up the app.

He shook his head at the irony. After everything this department had put him through, he had something that could possibly help them. And he was going to push aside his initial reaction of "let them fend for themselves" and do it.

This time they'd better not mess up.

TWO

An hour later, Ellen and Lee walked out of the building with Lee rolling the puppies behind in their carriers. "A dash cam?" Ellen asked him.

He shrugged. "I don't know. Call me paranoid. But after everything that happened with the crooked cop and…" He shook his head. "I'm not going to be in that position again. So I mounted a dash cam on my rearview mirror as some sort of protection, I guess. Maybe it was stupid."

"And maybe you're brilliant. I can't say I blame you a bit. And it allowed us to see one of the men in the car."

"Yes." He frowned.

"Everything all right?"

"Yes. I'm just thinking."

"About?" She spotted the SUV in the road, getting ready to turn in to the lot. "Hold that thought."

Whitney Godwin, also a rookie K-9 officer, pulled in and parked. She climbed out of the truck, her shoulder-length light blond hair blowing around her face. She shoved it back and waved at Ellen. "Hey, there. Are you okay?"

"We survived. That's the good news. Thanks for

bringing the car," Ellen said. "Lee picked me up at my home this morning so we're a bit stranded." She took the keys from Whitney's outstretched hand. Looking into her friend's eyes, she could see contentment. Happiness. All due to the new man in her life. A doctor named David Evans. They'd had some hard times but had made it through to the other side. Now they were planning a wedding.

It made Ellen happy for Whitney…and sad for herself. Would she ever have that look? She glanced at Lee. She'd actually had it years ago. Back when she and Lee were together. When they weren't fighting about her mother, they'd had some great times, been happy. She sighed. Whitney's features clouded in concern. "Why the heavy sigh? You okay?"

Ellen forced her lips into an upward curve. "Yes, just…reminiscing, sorry. Do you need a ride anywhere?"

"No." Whitney's smile came back. "David's on his way to get me. We're taking Shelby for a picnic." Shelby was Whitney's baby daughter.

Lee found a spot of grass, clipped leashes to the three pups and let them loose to take care of business. When they were finished, he got them back into the carriers and rolled them over to the vehicle where she and Whitney stood.

"Lee, do you know Whitney?"

He set the puppies in the back area of the vehicle where Carly usually rode, then held out a hand to Whitney. "I don't think we've met. It's a pleasure."

"Same here." She eyed the building and grimaced. "I hate to go in on my day off, but I have some leftover paperwork I need to finish up before David and I can enjoy the rest of the day. I'll see you later."

She disappeared through the glass doors. Lee turned to Ellen. "I'm starving," he said.

"Want to hit a drive-through and take the food to the training facility? We can eat and talk business if you're up to it."

"I am if you are."

He still looked a bit distracted. What was on his mind? The shooting probably. "You okay?"

He blinked and climbed into the passenger seat. "Yeah."

"Something's bothering you."

"How do you figure?"

She gave a low chuckle. "Come on, Lee, we used to be best friends." Actually, they'd been more than that, but that sentence was much safer than saying they'd one time been in love. The flare in his eyes said he was thinking it. She cleared her throat. "I can read you pretty well even after all these years. You have that little tic in your forehead that gives you away every time."

He pressed his fingers to it and his brow furrowed. "Let's get back to the facility so we can talk without distractions."

Ellen wasn't crazy about the fact that he wanted to wait to talk, but she could be patient. When she had to. But… "Why don't you just tell me what it is that's bothering you?"

He sighed. "Fine. When we were attacked, I thought I recognized one of the men in the car. The dash cam confirmed it."

Ellen stared at him even while she cranked the vehicle's ignition. "What? And you're just now saying something?"

"I wanted to know for sure before I said anything."

"And you're sure now?"

"No, but I figured you could help me find out if I'm right or not."

"So who do think it is?"

He sighed and rubbed his eyes. "I'm not sure so maybe I shouldn't say anything, but if it's him—"

Her ringing phone cut him off. She glanced at the dashboard. Chief Jones's number flashed. "Hello?"

Her Bluetooth kicked in and his voice came over the speakers. "Foxcroft. Where are you?"

"Just leaving the station. Do you need me to come back in?"

"No, just wanted to let you know we got a hit on that partial plate." While the chief talked, she drove.

"And?"

"There was a vehicle stolen last night. When we ran the partial against all of the ones in the system, we managed to narrow it down to the one that was used in the attack. Who knew you were going to pick up those puppies today?"

Ellen thought. "I don't know. It wasn't a secret. I've already checked with Lee and he didn't mention it to anyone. I told my staff at the assistance center so they could get an area prepared, but other than that, no one that I recall. Sophie could have mentioned it to someone, I suppose."

He grunted. "And it's possible the attack had nothing to do with that anyway. All right, rookie, be careful. Hopefully we'll get all this cleared up in the next day or so and you'll be back on duty. Tell Earnshaw the dash cam thing is paranoia at its finest. Glad he had it installed. Sorry he felt the need for it."

"He heard you."

"Thanks, Chief," Lee said before falling silent.

She hung up and within minutes, she was pulling into the parking lot of the Desert Valley Canine Assistance Center attached to the K-9 Unit Training Center.

Ellen threw the vehicle in Park and climbed out. Lee followed, rolling the puppies with him. He took them into a fenced area that had been specifically set up for them and let the three pups out of the carriers. They bolted into the warm grass, tumbling over one another, nipping and yapping, clearly glad to be able to run off some energy. "What are their names?" she asked. "They should be on their tags."

He pointed to the one running laps around the space. "That one is Dash."

"Appropriate." She looked at the other two. One sat on his haunches, tongue lolling as his gaze bounced between his friends. She walked over and snagged his tag. "This is King. I see why they named him that. He looks like a king ruling over his subjects."

"You're right, he does," Lee said with a nod. He grabbed the last dog by the collar as she wandered past and checked her tag. "And this is Lady."

She licked his hand and Ellen laughed. "Dainty and sweet."

He smiled. "All right. Dash, King and Lady. Poor girl is outnumbered, isn't she?"

"It'll make her stronger."

He nodded and locked the gate and walked toward her.

She waited for him, hands on her hips, mind only partially on naming the pups. She wanted to focus on what he'd revealed before the chief's call. "So you think you know one of the guys who attacked us?"

"Yes. A guy from the prison who was released around the same time I was."

She studied him. "What were you mixed up in at the prison, Lee, that would inspire someone to come after you like that?"

His jaw went rigid and Ellen blinked at the flare of rage—and hurt—that flashed in his eyes. "Really? That's the first thing that comes to you mind? That's what you think?" His fingers curled into fists. "You're just like her, aren't you?" he said, his voice low and strained.

"What?"

He jabbed a finger at her. "You're just like your mother."

"That's not fair."

"No, it's not. It's not fair that she didn't like me just because of who my family was. It's not fair that she interfered in our relationship. A lot of things aren't fair. And you're following right in her footsteps. You're judging me without all the facts. Well, that's fine. You're entitled to think and say what you want, but I don't have to stand here and listen to it." He started to walk off.

"Where are you going?"

"Home."

"How are you going to get there? You don't have a car, remember?"

He held up a cell phone, his eyes narrowed. She shivered at the coldness there. "All too well. However, while there aren't many, I do have a few friends left in this town. I can get a ride. Or I'll just walk. It's not that far." He spun on his heel and kept going.

Ellen sighed and dropped her chin to her chest. Was he right? Was she being judgmental? The fact that he compared her to her mother made her shudder. "Wait, Lee. Stop. You haven't even eaten your food."

"It's still in the bag, I'll take it with me."

He stopped his march at the car, opened the door and pulled out one of the fast-food bags. Then he turned his back on her once more and headed for the edge of her property, which would lead him to the main road. "Who was it, Lee? Who did you recognize?" He didn't answer, just kept walking. "Lee!"

"I'll talk to you tomorrow, Ellen." And then he disappeared around the edge of the house.

She gave a low groan and took off after him. "Stop, will you?"

She rounded the corner and slammed into his hard chest. "Oof."

He caught her biceps, the white food bag dangling from one hand. She looked up. The chill in his eyes hadn't thawed one degree. His features resembled granite. She drew in his scent and swallowed, the past rushing in to blindside her. She remembered clearly being held in his arms. Sitting in the hammock, her ear pressed against his chest, listening to his heart thud a steady beat. She remembered his sweet kisses and whispered promises. She remembered it all. And yearned to go back to recapture each and every moment.

He gently set her away from him and reality intruded. She straightened. There was no going back. There was only now and what the future might bring. And that didn't include Lee. Once the murders were solved and her mother woke from the coma—and she refused to believe she wouldn't—Ellen was going to request a transfer. There was no way she was staying Desert Valley forever. She was simply marking time until everything was wrapped up.

No matter what her mother thought—or wanted.

She was still leaving once the murders were solved. Ryder Hayes' wife's case was still open after five years, and the two deputies whose deaths originally looked like accidents now appeared to be possible murder victims. And so she and the other deputies were in Desert Valley until these cases were solved. But until then...

"Don't go," she blurted. Then bit her lip.

His eyes didn't soften—but he did hesitate. Hope flared. "I need to think about some things," he said, "and I need to do that at home. We'll talk later."

She sighed. When he was in this kind of mood there was no talking him out of it. "Fine. I'll give you a ride home. Let me get Carly."

He studied her a moment, then gave a terse nod. She walked up the steps to the front door, unlocked it and whistled for Carly. The sleek golden retriever with the soft brown eyes bounded over to her and expressed her delight in Ellen's presence. Ellen scratched the dog's silky ears then led the way to the truck. She opened Carly's door and the dog hopped in, sniffing the area. The pups had left their scent and Carly definitely noticed. She finally seemed to accept the smell and settled down. Ellen shut the door and climbed into the driver's seat. Lee was already in the truck with his seat belt fastened. "Will you at least tell me who you recognized? I need to know."

She started the truck and backed out of the spot. Lee considered keeping the information to himself, but couldn't do it. When she hit the main road, he finally answered her.

"A former inmate," he said. "And while he served at the same I did, I knew him before I went to prison." He winced. "Even after everything it still galls me to say that sentence." He tightened his jaw against the anger then breathed deeply before exhaling slowly. He could tell her this. He used to tell her everything. And even though he wasn't exactly happy with her jump to judgment, if he had information that could lead to Veronica's killer, he'd swallow his pride. "I used to hang out with him before I met you."

"So who is he?"

He sighed. "A troublemaker. Like I said, he was released about the same time I was. Not because he was innocent, but because he'd served his time."

"A name, Lee."

He sighed. "Freddie Parrish."

She lifted a brow. "Freddie Parrish? Wait a minute. I know him. We went to high school with him."

"Yep. He and I graduated together. I kind of lost track of him after high school, though. We went our separate ways."

"Yeah. You went to college."

"Yes."

"And so did Freddie, for a while. He had options. He could have finished school. He could have just gone to work if he didn't want to do school. I wonder what made him turn to a life of crime."

He shook his head. "Some people just make bad decisions, get mixed up with the wrong people. I don't know." He rubbed his chin. "You know, they offered a lot of college courses at the prison."

"Sure, I know that. Including the vet tech program through one of the local colleges in Flagstaff."

He nodded. "A lot of the inmates take advantage of it to get their education. It gives them hope that when they get out, they can stay straight and get a good job."

"I think it's a great idea."

"I know Freddie took a couple of the courses, and was even real close to finishing the program before he was recruited to work with the program's veterinarian, who took care of the puppies."

"What was he in prison for?" she asked.

"He had several DUIs and had gotten off with fines the first couple of times. Then he got into a bar fight with a guy who was supposed to be a friend and cut him with broken bottle. The judge gave him three years. He served all three."

She tapped the wheel. "We'll check him out, see if he has an alibi for the shooting." She handed him her phone. "Send a text to the chief with the information, will you? Tell him I want Freddie brought in for questioning."

Lee did as she'd asked.

She drove with confidence, and then he caught her looking at him from the corner of her eye. "What?" he asked.

"Don't take this the wrong way, but did you renew your friendship with Freddie in prison?"

Her question rocked him and he shot her a black look. "No, we didn't renew our friendship. The only reason I was ever around him was because he was a vet tech for the Prison Pups program. We worked together and that was it. I liked the program. Sophie Williams is a good woman and amazing with the dogs. I kept my mouth shut and my head down because I didn't want to lose out on the only thing that allowed me to forget—if just for a brief moment—what my life had become."

She swallowed and looked down. "I understand."

"No. You don't. And I hope you never do. Anyway, I caught Freddie mistreating the animals and told Sophie. She was furious and kicked him out of the program."

She pursed her lips and raised a brow. "I would think that might cause him to hold a grudge."

"Yes, but he doesn't strike me as the type to work alone."

"What do you mean?"

"He's a bully only when he feels like his victims won't—or can't—fight back or when he knows someone's got his back. In prison, during the time in the yard, he only hung around with those he'd earned favor with."

"Earned favor with?"

Lee sighed. "You've been in law enforcement long enough to know that prison has its own culture. There are rules and regulations just like on the outside, but they're tailored for prison life. It *looked* like Freddie was behaving himself. It *looked* like he was a model prisoner, but mostly that was because he was so sneaky. He never got caught doing anything wrong—until I caught him being rough with the pups. But he had access to areas of the prison that others didn't have. As a result, he was able to gather information that he could either use to gain favor with those who had more clout than himself or sell to the highest bidder."

"I see. He had friends who would watch his back so he could continue his sneaky activities. Friends that would do his dirty work if he needed them to."

"Exactly."

Ellen frowned. "Okay. Hopefully the chief will have

someone bring him—and whoever was with him—in for questioning soon."

"Hopefully." He rubbed a hand through his hair. "And now, if you don't mind, I'd like to change the subject," he said.

"All right. What is it?"

"I don't want *you* to take this the wrong way, but you cops are looking at the wrong people for suspects in Veronica's murder."

"What do you mean?"

"You're looking at the troublemakers, the people with grudges—and that's a list a mile long and is going to take forever to cover. You need to be looking at the not so obvious."

"We're running the investigation exactly as it's supposed to be run."

"I know that's what you think, but I'm not sure I agree." He held up a hand. "No, I'm not a cop and, no, I haven't been trained in criminal investigation, but I can't help thinking that you need to be looking at Veronica's last day. Who did she come into contact with? Who did she speak with? Interact with? Fight with?"

Ellen pulled up at his house and simply sat while she digested his words. He watched her mull them over and knew she was formulating a response to appease him. He let her think while he looked at his home trying to see it through her eyes.

He loved what he'd managed to do with it. Now it had an outbuilding attached to a kennel. The exercise areas were fenced in and ready to see action. He'd built a good business before he'd been incarcerated.

His gaze wandered to the small three-bedroom ranch house that he'd grown up in. One her mother considered to be on the wrong side of town, but one where he knew Ellen had found acceptance and many hours of happiness—as long as Veronica wasn't home. They'd all been happier when his sister hadn't been home. Guilt hit him at the thought and he grimaced.

"I hear what you're saying, Lee, I do," Ellen said. "And we're looking into all of that. I promise we're doing our job."

"I'm not saying you're not. I'm simply saying your focus is in the wrong place. Ordinary people can snap when pushed too far, not just the troublemakers." He'd learned that in prison.

She sighed. "I don't know what else to tell you. We're aware of this. We're working on it. Investigations take time." She tapped her fingers on the wheel. "Okay, I'll tell you this." She paused.

"Tell me what?"

"One thing that's really got our attention is the break-ins that are happening all around town. I'm sure you've heard of them."

"Yes, of course." Everyone in town was on edge due to the break-ins.

"There's been a rash of them," she said. "Residents are worried and so are the cops. We understand their need to protect their property and their families, but we also don't need a trigger-happy home owner accidentally shooting his neighbor."

He grunted and climbed from the truck. "A valid concern. On both sides. But what do the break-ins have to do with the investigation into my sister's murder?"

"They're not your average, run-of-the-mill break-ins. The people doing them don't steal anything. Yes, if there's some cash lying around, they take it, but they don't steal expensive electronics that could be easily fenced or even things like jewelry. One woman had a thousand-dollar diamond necklace hanging on her mirror and they left it."

"Maybe they just didn't notice it."

"That's possible. But it's not just that. This just *feels* different. It's like they're looking for something and when they don't find it, they just leave."

"So what are they looking for?" He'd forgotten his anger with her for the moment, simply glad she was sharing the information with him.

"When we found your sister, we also found her with two German shepherd pups. We know she was planning on microchipping three."

"Yes, I know all that." He'd been told this when he'd gone to the station after his release from prison demanding answers about the progress in his sister's investigation. "Hold that thought. Grab your food and let's eat inside."

She snagged the bag and released Carly. The dog sniffed the ground as she followed the humans toward the house. Ellen stepped inside his childhood home. She looked around. "I heard about your dad dying. I'm so sorry."

Lee closed his eyes. "I am, too. Even sorrier that he drank himself to death and there wasn't anything I could do to stop him." He cleared his throat and moved aside a stack of magazines from the kitchen table. "Veronica kept the house up for me while I was incarcerated. As much as I hated this place growing up—with the exception of the times that you were here—I sure was glad to have it to come back to when I got out a couple of weeks ago."

"I'm sure." She looked at the dog. "Carly, sit." Carly's hind end hit the floor. "Good girl." She scratched her ears.

He pulled the food out of the bag and set it on the table. "Water okay? I don't have much to drink around here."

"Water sounds great." He filled the glasses and a bowl for Carly. The dog lapped it and Lee joined her at the table. "So enough about that. You said you found Veronica with two puppies, but she was supposed to be microchipping three."

"Right. We still haven't found the missing puppy, Marco."

He lifted a brow. "I've seen the signs around town, the posters asking for information. Is he really that important to the case?"

"We believe so. And we believe the person who killed your sister is the one breaking in to the houses. We think they're looking for that missing German shepherd puppy, as well."

He frowned. "But…why?" He took a bite out of his hamburger and shook a few fries onto the wrapper.

"We don't know," Ellen said. "Unless the people who broke in to the K-9 training center were after the puppies in the first place. Maybe they wanted them to sell." She shrugged. "Veronica was there microchipping those puppies as a last-minute thing. Maybe the people who broke in to the training center thought she would be gone. We don't know. We haven't put it all together yet, but the missing puppy is definitely a connection in your sister's murder."

He rubbed his eyes. "Thanks for telling me that. It helps to know there's at least one lead you're following."

"So…" She cleared her throat. "I'm sorry."

"For?"

"Judging you. I shouldn't have reacted like that. I'm sure while you were in prison you came across a lot of troublemakers. Troublemakers you'd recognize once they were back on the street." She shook her head. "I jumped to conclusions. I was wrong and I'm sorry for hurting you. Again."

A lump formed in his throat and he looked away for a moment to get his emotions under control. He took a sip of water. "It's hard not to get defensive sometimes. I'm working on it. I worked on it for the entire two years I was locked up for something I didn't do. I watched my father become a bitter, hateful man after my mother walked out. Veronica changed, too. She went from being a loving sister to a nasty person I didn't want to be around for very long. I determined at a young age that I wouldn't let life do that to me." He gave a low laugh. "I never thought life would throw an undeserved prison sentence at me, though, so it's been a struggle to keep that promise to myself, but my grandmother's influence, her unwavering support, visits—and prayers—have helped."

"I'm sure. Your grandmother was a sweetheart."

He nodded. "Still is." He glanced at his plate. "She's living in a retirement home now in Flagstaff and is loving it. I'm happy for her. I wish I could get down there more often to visit, though." Flagstaff was about four hours south of Desert Valley. Lee took another sip of his drink and set the glass on the table. "You have some big plans for the assistance center. I like the way you think."

She raised a brow. "Well, thanks." Her eyes started to glow. "You know, coming from a wealthy background was often a pain when I was growing up. Everyone thought my life should be perfect because I was a Fox-

croft. Didn't matter that my parents fought all the time
or that, when my father finally left, my mother started
micromanaging my life."

"I know your life wasn't perfect."

"Yes, you understood more than the average person.
At first when I graduated from the K-9 training center and was given this assignment, I was furious." She
twisted the napkin between her fingers. "To be honest,
I actually thought about quitting."

"What?" He stared. "Why?"

She shrugged. "Well, it was only a brief thought. But
I didn't want to be back under my mother's heavy thumb.
I was afraid if I came back to Desert Valley, I would…
ah…revert to my wimpy high school self, I suppose."

He tilted his head. "But you haven't."

"No." Her jaw tightened.

"So why did you move back in with her?"

Ellen sighed and pinched the bridge of her nose. "I
didn't really want to, but…she played on my guilt."

"How so?"

"Oh, you know. She was so glad I was staying in
town, she went on and on about how worried she'd been
about me going off and being a cop in a strange place
and how she was so lonely." Ellen sighed. "It was just
supposed to be a temporary thing. I told her I'd move
back until I found a place to stay."

"Why didn't you stay with the other officers? In the
apartment for the rookies?" The apartment had been part
of the program, set up to house all the trainees during
their sessions. Now that the town was in the midst of a
crime wave and the latest group of rookies were staying
in town, the apartment had been opened up for them to

continue living there should they choose to do so. Some had, but not Ellen.

She grimaced. "I felt like it would be a slap in my mother's face, so I sucked it up and moved in with her." Her eyes narrowed. "However, when I learned I was coming back here for an extended period of time, I was determined I would do something good with all that money sitting in the bank."

"Hence the assistance program."

"Yes."

"It's an awesome use of the money, Ellen. The assistance program is very much needed and not just in Desert Valley—you'll be touching lives all over the country. There are never enough trained animals to go out to those in need."

"I know. I've been thinking about that. If this thing gets up and running like I hope it will, the center could always expand as needed."

"I agree. Expanding would be great. And I have an idea of what we'll need in order to consider that at some point in the future."

"What do you have in mind?"

"I've been meaning to discuss this with you and just haven't had the chance. We had talked about ways to get the community involved in the center and, like we discussed, I have several tours of the space lined up. Some politicians, some families and some school groups. In spite of the money you've put into it, I think we should let the public give to it, as well. When people give money to a cause, they tend to pay attention to it and hold it close to their heart. We need that from the good folks in Desert Valley. Once we have that, we can think about other areas."

She nodded. "That's a great idea." She smiled and his heart warmed. "You've done all of that in such a short time. That's impressive." She reached across and grasped his fingers. "I'm so thankful you said yes to working with me, Lee. You're an amazing addition to the team."

He felt the heat rise in his cheeks but focused on the feel of her warm hand on his. Her touch reminded him of the past, of the days they'd laughed and held hands as though their time together was as long as eternity. "Thanks." His voice came out husky and he cleared his throat. "And I think your summer camp idea is a fabulous one, too." She'd gone into detail about that when she'd hired him. "We won't be able to do many weeks this summer, maybe the first two weeks of August before school starts back, but next year we should be able to get off to an immediate start when the school year is over."

Ellen stilled and went quiet. Then gave a slow nod. "Yes, next year."

"What is it?"

She blew out a low breath and shook her head. "Nothing, nothing. Your ideas are wonderful. Your long-term planning is amazing and a real benefit to the program."

"But?"

She sighed. "But I don't know where I'll be in a year."

His heart dropped and he cleared his throat. "I…ah,… I see. So what does that mean?"

"Lee, I'm not hanging around here. I'm doing my best to get away from Desert Valley." *And my mother.* He heard the words even though she didn't say them out loud. Which meant she'd be leaving him, too. Again. "And as soon as we solve Veronica's murder," she continued, oblivious to his aching heart, "my assignment is complete and I'm free to move on to another city. Or state."

He gave a slow nod. "Okay then. Thanks for the heads up." And the warning to guard his heart. The one that was beating a sad rhythm as he tried to reign in his emotions. He fell silent for a moment then sighed. "At least when—if—you decide to go somewhere else, you'll be leaving behind a legacy that will continue to help people for a very long time." Because while he intended to finish vet school, he could see himself returning to Desert Valley to continue working with the program. Maybe even as the program's full-time vet.

Maybe.

The thought of doing all of that without Ellen by his side left a bitter taste in his mouth. He pulled his hand from under hers and returned to his food. For the next few minutes an uncomfortable silence hovered between them.

Ellen finished her dinner and stood. "I should get going. I need to go by the hospital and check on my mother." She tossed the wrappers into the trash can, then glanced at her phone. "I know if there was any change in her condition, they would call me, but sometimes I hope that just by my being there, she'll know it. That it might trigger something in her brain and she'll wake up. Even if it's the desire to tell me I'm ruining my life." She gave him a rueful smile.

"You're a good daughter."

The smile slipped off and her jaw tightened. "Too good sometimes, I'm afraid. And not good enough at other times." She looked into his eyes and Lee's heart beat a little faster at what he saw there. "I have regrets, Lee, I just want you to know that. I really do."

He reached out a hand and dragged a finger down her soft cheek. He knew what she was referring to. "I do, too. Unfortunately, I don't think it's possible to go through life and not acquire a few regrets." He sighed and pulled her into a hug. She stiffened then relaxed and let him hold her. It hit home how much he'd missed her. "I'm sorry you're having to go through this."

"Thanks, me too." She sucked in a deep breath and pulled back. His arms immediately felt empty but he didn't protest. "Do you need me to come get you in the morning?" she asked.

"I suppose. I'll need to get a rental car, I guess."

"You can use one of my mother's cars. She has a Jeep and a BMW. I recommend the Jeep."

"Um, no way, thanks. If Marian Foxcroft wakes up and finds that you've let me drive one of her vehicles, she'll have both of us arrested for grand theft auto. I'll pass on that one."

"Ha-ha. She will not." *She might try, though.* "I have some pull with the police around here should she try anything. Seriously, I should have thought of it before I brought you home, but we'll take care of it tomorrow."

He was touched by her offer. Mostly because he hadn't been expecting it. Still… "I really don't think it's a good idea."

"Well, I do. End of discussion."

Lee drew in a deep breath. "Okay, if you're sure."

"I am."

"Then…I'd appreciate it. I'll call George at the body shop first thing in the morning and see when he thinks he'll have my truck ready. Might be a while, though."

"That's fine. I'll come get you in the morning."

He nodded and stood to walk her out the door. A

low thud made him pause. He looked at Ellen. "Did you hear that?"

Carly rose to her feet, ears cocked, attention on the front door. "I did and so did she." Ellen lifted a finger to her lips and pulled her weapon. "Stay here. Someone's out there."

THREE

Ellen motioned for Lee to step back into the protection of the kitchen area. He frowned but followed her silent order. "Carly, heel." Carly was at her side in a split second. She would stay right there until commanded to do otherwise. Ellen moved to the side window, staying away from the front of the door, and gently moved the curtain so she could see out.

Nothing. She flipped the porch light off, then let her eyes adjust. When nothing happened, her nerves tightening with each second, she eased the deadbolt to the right and slowly opened the door. Darkness greeted her. Stillness. At least no one shot at her.

Yet. Carly nudged her leg, her ears perked forward, attention on the outside.

"Who's there?" Ellen called.

Again, nothing.

And yet Carly nearly vibrated.

She caught Lee's eye. His frown deepened and he shook his head when he realized she meant to step outside. She frowned right back, moved out the door and slipped to the side, pressing her back against the wall of the house. She waited for Carly to pad out, then used her left hand to slowly shut the door. It was the best she could do to make herself as small a target as possible. She stood there, listening. Silence. No sound. Nothing that alarmed her.

She moved toward the steps, then froze when she heard a rustle to her left. She spun, lifting her weapon, wishing she had on her vest. But she could see nothing.

But her senses told her someone was out there. Watching. The hair spiked on the back of her neck. "Police! Who's there? Show yourself," she called. Then moved quickly in case someone decided to shoot in the direction of her voice.

But no bullets came her way.

Carly stayed right at her side, waiting for the command that would send her after whoever was hiding. But Ellen wasn't ready to do that yet. As long as her own life wasn't in danger, she wouldn't let the dog go in blind. Ellen moved down the steps and out into the yard, taking cover behind the nearest tree. Her heart thundered in her ears.

Should she call for backup?

But no one had done anything yet. A flash of light in the direction of the kennel pulled her attention. She hesitated only for a moment. "Carly, seek," she said and pointed.

Carly took off like a shot. Ellen moved quickly, following behind the animal. Sweat trickled down her back. She drew in shallow breaths and reached for her phone.

The sound of running footsteps just ahead of her reached her ears. She stayed behind Carly and whoever she was chasing only to stop when she heard an engine turn over and then a slight squeal of tires as the vehicle sped off into the night. At the edge of the road,

Ellen bent and placed her hands on her knees. She took
a long breath. Carly barked twice then settled at Ellen's
side. "Got away, didn't he, girl?" Ellen slipped the dog
a treat and Carly wolfed it down, proud of herself. Ellen
scratched her ears and straightened when she heard footsteps.

"Ellen?"

She spun to find Lee behind her, only slightly winded.
"What are you doing? Trying to get yourself killed?"

"Sorry, I had to make sure you were all right."

"I can take care of myself. That's what I'm trained
for, remember?"

Again her words caused a flash of hurt to darken his
features. She sighed. She was tired. It had been a long
day. But that was no excuse to snap at the man and hurt
his feelings. "Again, I'm sorry. I can't seem to get the
filters to line up with my tongue." She paused. "I appreciate the concern. Next time it might best if you stay
back, though."

The mask fell away and he barked a short laugh. "You
don't have to pretty it up for me, Ellen. You've always
been blunt. No sense in trying to change now."

She felt the heat rush into her cheeks. "Well, when
you put it that way…fine. Do you have a flashlight?"

"You want me to turn the floodlights on? Or would
that put us in the spotlight?"

She hesitated. "I think whoever was snooping out here
is gone, but we probably don't want to make it any easier
to spot us should the person double back. I'm nervous
enough standing here in the moonlight."

"Gotcha."

Because while she'd heard the person drive away and

Carly no longer seemed concerned, Ellen felt the need to take all kinds of precautions.

Still worried that the intruder might return, Lee entered the kennel where he used to keep the dogs he'd loved to work with. That was before he'd had to make other arrangements for them when he was sentenced to prison. Veronica had helped him out with that. He even knew that a couple of them were now working dogs, trained by his sister's skilled hand and rehomed to help those who needed it. Anger at all he'd lost surged through him and he had to squelch it before it grew.

That was in the past, he reminded himself. He had a future now. A future that included this home, this kennel that he'd built with his own two hands in his backyard. Thankfully, Veronica had hired someone to keep the outside area cut and trimmed while she took care of the house herself. He supposed the house hadn't been much work since no one was living there. Simply dust and vacuum once a week. His backyard had been another matter, though. And while this area might be empty at the moment, he hoped to fill it up soon with more puppies to train for people who needed them. After all, he still had the rest of his schooling to pay for.

One step at a time.

They'd left the puppies at the training center, so tomorrow he'd get the one golden retriever pup from Ellen. Dash. That little one seemed to need a bit more of his expertise than the other two. He grabbed the flashlight he'd come for and hurried back outside to find Ellen making notes on her phone. "You're going to report this?"

"Yes. We need to keep everything documented. I don't want whoever is doing this to slip through our fingers on a technicality. I've got the date, time and description of what I heard and saw—and Carly's reaction, as well."

He handed her the flashlight and she clipped the phone to her belt then flipped the light on. She aimed the beam toward the ground. "Follow me and let's use both sets of eyes. You may spot something that shouldn't be there before I would. Carly will let us know if anyone comes back."

He moved closer to her. Drew in her familiar scent. He used to dream about that smell while he was in prison— and even before. A combination of vanilla and strawberries. He was glad some things hadn't changed.

Even while his mind remembered, his eyes scoured the ground. They worked in a grid pattern. Up toward the road, then back. Finally, he pointed. "There. Near the gate." She moved closer and aimed the light where he indicated. "The grass is pressed down. I've been meaning to get out here and cut it, but haven't had a chance. With the rain a couple of days ago, it seems like it grew about a foot overnight."

She pulled her phone off the clip and snapped pictures. "I don't know what good the pictures will do. There aren't any footprints to cast or anything like that, but I see what you mean about the grass."

Her light flashed across something shiny in the grass and he bent down to pick it up then stopped. "Do you have a tissue or gloves or anything?"

"Not on me." She moved closer and looked over his shoulder. Her nearness made him long for things he shouldn't. She wasn't going to be around any longer than it took to solve his sister's murder. He needed to remember that. "I wasn't planning on working a crime scene," she said, oblivious to his inner turmoil. Good, he planned to keep it that way. "What is it?"

He drew in a breath and forced his thoughts to the object on the ground. "It's the clip that keeps the gate closed. Some of the dogs can figure out how to lift the latch so I just use the clip. Someone undid it and gave it a toss." He stood. "Be right back. I've got some paper towels and paper bags in the room I used to use as an office."

He left her once again to retrieve the items. When he returned, he handed her a paper towel and she scooped up the clip and slid it in the bag. "We'll send this off to Flagstaff and have them try to find any prints," she said. "If the person wore gloves, it'll be a lost cause."

"Thanks. It's worth a try."

"If I were to go inside the gate, where could I get to?"

"Just inside the building I used as a kennel. It's got some cages and dog runs out the back. I would put the dogs inside when the weather was too cold or too hot for them to be outside. But I keep the door leading into the actual building locked. There's nothing worth stealing in there—just pet food, a few tools, water buckets, training toys…" He shrugged. "It's really just a storage area."

"This makes me nervous," Ellen said. "Someone shot at us today and now someone is snooping around your home tonight. I don't like it."

"I can't say it's been the highlight of my week, either."

She sighed. "All right. Let's go back to the house. I want to make some phone calls."

He led the way back into his kitchen. She settled into a chair with Carly at her feet and dialed a number.

"Who are you calling?"

"Two other K-9 officers in my unit. Tristan McKeller and Shane Weston. I'm going to ask them to take turns watching your house tonight." She bit her lip. "I suppose I should call Chief Jones, too."

While she made the calls, he rubbed his eyes and considered the past few hours. He had to admit he hadn't realized what he was signing up for when he'd agreed to work with Ellen. He hadn't realized how much the past would come back to haunt him. How much he would wish for what could never be. He watched her talk, examining her face, her expressions, her intensity. Beautiful, ambitious, smart… He sighed. And what was he?

Before he'd been arrested and imprisoned, he'd had big dreams. He'd been building his dog-training business and even had two college students who'd worked for him on a part-time basis. He'd also been attending graduate classes that would get him started on the path to becoming a veterinarian. And then he'd walked into a convenience store in the middle of a robbery. The clerk had been shot and he'd tried to save her. The robber had fled, and Officer Ken Bucks had arrived on the scene. Just in time to set him up. He'd held a grudge against Lee ever since a woman Ken loved had chosen Lee over him. Ken had never forgotten it—nor cared that Lee hadn't returned the woman's affection.

The anger bubbled, threatening to come to the surface once again. He blew out a sigh.

Why was he going down that path again? It was in the past. He couldn't change what happened. He'd been in the wrong place at the wrong time with the wrong cop—and while the woman had lived, she hadn't seen who'd shot her. The jury hadn't believed Lee's defense in the face of all of the evidence Bucks had managed to gather. False evidence. Manipulated evidence. Like altering the video footage.

"Lee? You okay?"

He jerked at Ellen's question, then followed her gaze to see his fingers curled into tight fists. He relaxed them. "Yes, thanks. What did you find out?"

While he could still see the concern in her eyes, she didn't question him further. "Both officers can help out. Tristan has a fourteen-year-old sister he's raising, but she's spending the night with a friend so he's free for the first six-hour shift. Then Shane will take over."

"Not having had the best experience when it comes to dealing with cops, I have to say I appreciate their help."

"You got a raw deal with Ken Bucks. It's time you realize we're not all cut from the same cloth." She smiled.

"I realize it. If you trust them, then I do, too."

"I trust them. With my life."

"That's good enough for me, then."

When Tristan arrived, Ellen introduced them and Lee sized up the rookie who was not just a member of the unit, but a good friend to Ellen. Lee felt a twinge of jealousy, but mostly he was glad she'd done well with her life and had people she could count on when she needed to. He wasn't sure he could say the same.

She grabbed her keys. "I'll be leaving now. Tristan, would you mind asking Shane to drop Lee at the training center in the morning? His truck is out of commission. I was going to come get him, but Shane'll be heading that way."

It didn't escape his attention that she'd just gotten out of picking him up. And that his feelings were hurt by it.

"Happy to ask," Tristan said, "but you and I both know it won't be an issue."

"Thanks."

Lee pushed aside the hurt. Maybe she had her reasons

for not wanting to swing by and get him. He nodded to his Keurig coffeemaker and the K-Cup tree next to it. The tree held about five different flavored coffees. The Keurig and the coffee had been one of the first things he purchased after he was released from prison. A splurge he hadn't regretted for a moment.

"Help yourself."

Tristan didn't hesitate and Ellen smiled. "You just made a friend for life."

Lee walked to the door but stayed away from the windows. Ellen followed him. "Be careful. You were with me when everything happened. If Freddie thinks we can ID him, he'll be looking for you, too."

"I'll keep that in mind."

He turned to look at her. "Why did you choose to become a cop? You were determined to be a doctor from what I remember," he said. "What changed?"

She sighed. "It's a long story. The short version is that a friend of mine and I were almost mugged. She was a karate instructor. She defended us, took down the guy and held him until the cops got there. As soon as we were safe and I had a chance to process everything, I knew that if she hadn't been there, or if she hadn't had the training she'd had, the night would have ended a lot differently. And plus, I was mad. I decided I wanted to be the one to protect others, to catch the bad guys, to defend those who can't defend themselves."

"I can imagine how your mother reacted to that one. From medical school to the police academy would be quite the step down in her eyes."

"Yes, you're right about that. I didn't tell her at first." She shrugged. "Finally, I had no choice and after a rant or two, she…adjusted."

"I can't see that."

"Okay, so…she's still adjusting. I have hopes. Now I've got to go." She glanced at her phone's screen. "I'm not going to make the hospital tonight. Give me some time to make a morning visit. See you around ten at the center?"

"I'll go ahead and get there whenever Shane's ready. That way I can start working with the pups."

She rubbed her eyes and stifled a yawn. "That's settled, then. I'll see you in the morning." She started toward her SUV, Carly at her side. Then she stopped and spun. "Actually, do you mind answering one more question? It's been on my mind for a while now."

Wary, he shrugged. "What?"

"Why did Ken Bucks hate you so much?"

He flinched. "You sure you want to hear that tonight?"

"The short version."

"That's all there is anyway." He raked a hand through his already mussed hair. "Do you remember Shelley Graves?"

"Yes. She was a little older than you, wasn't she?"

"Yes. Three years older. Anyway, Ken decided he was in love with her and followed her around like a lovesick puppy, wrote her notes, parked outside her house to watch her come and go. All kinds of crazy stuff."

She blinked. "Okay. So what does that have to do with you?"

He sighed and looked away. He really didn't want to remember that time but he'd tell her the story and be done with it. "About four years ago, Ken was still after her. He'd never given up on her even after all those years."

"She never married?"

"No. And she and her boyfriend had called it quits after someone left threatening messages at his house."

"Ken was stalking her."

"Yeah. One afternoon, I ran into Shelley at the Cactus Café and she invited me to sit at her table. She was nervous and looked upset. I felt sorry for her so I sat with her. She started telling me what was going on and asked me what she should do. I told her she needed to go to the chief and tell him what Ken was doing." He blew out a breath. "But she was afraid to. After all, Ken was the chief's stepson, right?"

"Yes, I knew that."

"Anyway, Ken came in about the time we finished eating and came to the table. He tried to pick a fight with me, but there was no way I was going there. I could see the headlines: Local Dog Trainer and Vet Wannabe Assaults Deputy Sheriff."

She grimaced. "Ouch."

"Anyway, I simply told Ken to leave her alone."

"How did he take that?"

"I thought he was going to spontaneously combust." He grimaced. "Anyway, after that, Shelley started to look at me like I was some kind of hero or something. One evening, she came over to my house. She told me she was in love with me and had come to convince me that I felt the same way about her. When I told her that I didn't return her affection, she kissed me. I immediately stepped away from her, but the damage was done."

"Oh, my."

"Apparently Ken had followed her to my place and… uh…he saw the whole thing."

"Oh, no."

"Oh, yes." His lips tightened. "He's hated me ever since."

"But you moved away from her."

"I did, but he didn't stay to see that part. From then on, he became more snide and rude. He even stopped me one night and harassed me. Made me take a breathalyzer test and all that. Gave me a ticket for going five miles over the speed limit." He shook his head. "I filed a formal complaint with Chief Jones, but I don't know that he ever did anything. The harassment stopped so that was good. I managed to steer pretty clear of him until the night of the robbery."

"And he held on to that grudge all that time," she whispered.

"Yep. All that time. And when the robbery went down and I was there—" Lee shrugged, fighting the emotions the memories brought to the surface "—he finally found a way to get me back."

"Unbelievable."

"You would think so."

"What happened to Shelley?"

"She wound up moving to New Mexico with a friend. She's a nurse and is working at one of the hospitals there."

Ellen walked back to him and wrapped her arms around his waist to hug him. "I'm so sorry, Lee. You didn't deserve that."

He almost couldn't speak through the tightness in his throat, but managed a husky "Thanks. And I guess that was more the long version than short. Sorry."

"No apologies necessary. See you tomorrow."

And then she was walking away again. Carly trotted at her heels then jumped into her space in the truck.

Ellen shut the door then climbed in the driver's seat. He heard her truck rumble to life and then the tires crunch on the gravel after the concrete ran out. He sighed and went back inside, making his way into the kitchen.

"Women, huh?"

Lee schooled his features and looked at Tristan, who'd made himself at home at the kitchen table. "What?"

Tristan shook his head. "I'm right there with you, man. Trying to understand them is like trying to understand a foreign language with no training. I've got custody of my fourteen-year-old sister and I can't seem to do or say anything right. Just yesterday I told her what a pretty young woman she was turning into and she started crying. Big old sobs that threatened to rip the heart right out of me." He shook his head. "I don't understand her, that's for sure."

"Sounds like you're on the right path, then."

Tristan grunted and Lee ran a hand down the side of his face. "I'm exhausted. I'm going to get a shower and head to bed. You need anything?"

Tristan lifted the coffee mug. "I've got all I need."

Lee nodded. "Well, there's more where that came from. Help yourself. I probably won't see you before you leave, so thank you for doing this."

"Absolutely."

Lee headed for his bedroom at the back of the house. His footsteps echoed on the wood floors. He checked each window, and when he was satisfied his home was as secure as possible, he finally allowed himself to relax and dream about returning to school one day. He was financially set whenever he decided to go back. While he'd been in prison, Veronica had handled his money and had done a good job with what little he'd had. She'd in-

vested it and when he'd gotten his statements, he'd been
impressed with her ingenuity. He'd also been surprised
and grateful. Somewhere under that sarcastic, nasty personality she'd shown to the world, Lee wanted to believe
there'd still been a part of the sweet older sister who'd
looked out for him.

And he'd learned soon after her death that Veronica
had left everything to him in her will. He had enough
money to live on whenever he was able to return to
school, which was nice. But going to school would re-
quire him to leave Desert Valley, and he wasn't ready
to do that yet. Not with Veronica's murderer still running free. He'd return to school when the time was right.
Which reminded him that it wasn't right. Not with the
shooting that had happened. And the person on his property. And the fact that his heart was once again leaning
toward Ellen's.

All of that combined to make the tension come roaring
back, and he knew he wouldn't be sleeping much at all.

Ellen stepped into the home she'd grown up in, kicked
off her boots and released her belt with her weapon, set-
ting it on the coffee table. The mansion echoed around
her and she wished someone else were here. Like her
mother. Because it would mean she was whole and
healthy.

Carly nudged her as though reading her mind, and she
scratched the dog's ears, suddenly not feeling quite so
lonely. But the big house felt weird without her mother's
commanding presence. Her father hadn't been around
for years. She missed him and wished she could pick
up the phone and call him, but her mother had chased
him off, too, with her dictatorial personality. And then

he'd died a broken, lonely man. First her father, then her relationship with Lee had crashed and burned because her mother had had the audacity to publicly call Lee out and tell him he wasn't good enough for her daughter...

The anger burned deep inside her. Ellen cleared her throat and refused to go that route.

She called the hospital and checked on her mother.

"There's no change, Ms. Foxcroft," the nurse said. "She's still sleeping and healing. She's not in pain. She'll wake up when her body is ready."

Her shoulders sagged at the answer that never seemed to vary. It definitely was not what she wanted to hear, but it was better than her mother taking a turn for the worse. With everything in her, she didn't want her mother to die. Especially not with all of the unresolved issues between them. She bit back the rush of tears and headed for the shower.

And for the first time in days had a real chance to think about the one person whose footprint had never faded from her heart. Lee Earnshaw. He made her head spin and her heart long for things better left forgotten. He also made the guilt sweep in. She should have had more faith in him. She should have gone to see him in prison. But she hadn't. She'd thought about it. One time, she'd even made it to the parking lot of the prison before turning around and going home.

Why?

Because it had felt like a betrayal. She'd loved him and he'd turned to a life of crime. What had hurt the most was having to admit her mother had been right about him. *He's a loser, Ellen. He'll never amount to anything. You're too good for him.* Her mother's words rang in her ears and once Lee had been arrested, she'd finally had to admit that while the evidence was solid, she'd had a very hard time accepting Lee could be guilty of such a thing.

Self-loathing assaulted her. He hadn't been guilty. He'd been framed, and she'd just…gone about her life.

And thought about him every day. She should have visited him, believed in him, supported him.

But the evidence had just been overwhelming…

Her mother had wasted no time in letting Ellen know about the arrest: *I told you so.*

It had been depressing. So Ellen had moved out and moved on in spite of her mother's vociferous protests. Ellen had made a life for herself apart from her mother, apart from Desert Valley. And she'd had no intention of coming back. Only it looked as though God had other plans. She sighed.

She had a murder to solve. Well, more than one, really. K-9 officer Ryder Hayes's wife, Melanie, had been killed five years ago and her murderer had never been caught. Then Brian Miller and Mike Riverton, two rookie officers with the Desert Valley Police Department had been killed a year apart. Their deaths had been ruled accidents, but Tristan had been friends with Mike, served in the army with him and said he didn't believe for a minute that Mike had fallen down his steps to his death. And then exactly one year later, to the day, Brian had died in his home when it caught fire due to an unattended candle. That in itself was enough to raise the suspicions of those who knew him. His entire family had died in a fire when he was just a teen, and he never used candles or his fireplace. So the consensus was that the deaths had been made to look like accidents. But why? And who wanted them dead?

Ellen slipped between her sheets and Carly settled herself at the foot of her bed. So much death, Ellen thought. She just prayed neither she nor Lee would be next.

FOUR

Lee opened the passenger door and climbed out of Shane Weston's vehicle. "Thanks for the ride."

Shane nodded. "Not a problem."

Lee turned to find Ellen standing at the entrance to the training center. She'd arrived before him after all. A large boxer with a gray muzzle sat at her side. "Good morning," she said. "Did you get any rest last night?"

"A bit. You?"

"A bit." She motioned him inside, and he followed her into the lobby area where she had the three pups running free. The puppies chose that moment to playfully attack the boxer, who flopped onto the floor. He patiently let them climb all over him.

Then the smallest pup made a beeline for the area behind the front desk. Ellen snagged him and lifted him.

"Dash," Lee said.

"Yep."

The puppy licked her chin. Lee smiled and scratched its silky head. "He's living up to his name." She handed him the wriggling pup. "Who's your friend?" he asked.

"This is Kipper. He was waiting for me when I got

here this morning. A family pet no one had time for anymore."

He scowled. "Some people shouldn't have pets."

"I agree, but at least they brought him to me and didn't leave him abandoned on the side of the road somewhere."

"True." He looked around. "I can't get over how great this place is. I remember it being an empty building just sitting here waiting for someone to come along and give it life again."

"Thanks. I couldn't believe Veronica agreed to let me move my center in here. I don't think she ever really liked me that much."

"Veronica didn't like anyone very much."

"She loved you."

"Yes, I guess she did. In her own way. When we could talk about animals and training, we were on the same wavelength. If I tried to confront her about her immoral activities or vicious treatment of people, she froze me out." He shook his head. "The only reason I even believed we could possibly be related was because of the animals and her rapport with them." He sighed. "It's too bad she didn't use some of that talent with the humans in her life."

"I agree." She gave him a small smile. "I've got to make a call to see what my status is and if I'm cleared to go back to work. Why don't you take the puppies into the training area outside? I'll catch up to you after I finish my call and then we can go pick up the Jeep for you to use until your truck is ready."

He nodded. "That still makes me nervous, but as long as you're willing to take the fall, I'm willing to go along."

She laughed. "I'm willing."

"All right, then." He headed for the back area and

placed the puppies in the yard. He then walked over to where Ellen kept the treats for rewards. After shoving a handful into his front pocket, he got to work with Dash.

"Come on, boy. Sit." He tapped the puppy's hind end and pressed until he sat. The he slipped him a treat. "Good job, boy. Good job."

When Ellen emerged from the building an hour later, he realized he was sweltering and thirsty. He'd been giving the puppy water at regular intervals but had forgotten to bring himself something. He motioned to the air-conditioned building. She held out a water bottle, which he gladly took. "Thanks." They walked inside and he downed half of it. He gave the other half to the puppy, who eagerly finished it off.

"How's it going?" she asked when he came up for air.

Lee swiped his mouth and chin with the edge of his T-shirt and grinned when she wrinkled her nose. "We have towels inside, you know."

"It's a guy thing."

She gave a light snort. "Oh, I know."

"And in answer to your question, they're doing great. Especially King. He sure likes food."

"Good, should make him pretty easy to train."

"I think so. Dash might be another story. I got him to follow through a couple of times, and other times he acted like I was speaking Greek."

"He'll get it."

"Yes, he will." He went to the sink attached to the building and washed his hands. When he turned he found Ellen with Lady cradled against her. "So I never asked. How was your mother this morning?"

Sadness pulled her lips into a frown. "The same."

"I'm sorry. Are the doctors still offering hope that she'll wake up?"

"Yes, they seem to think she will. They just say that her brain needs time to heal."

"Do you think she saw who attacked her?"

"I don't know. That's why there's a guard on her 24/7. Just in case the person is afraid she did and comes back to finish the job." Her lips tightened. "I really want to find who did this."

"So you think there's any connection to all of the other stuff going on in town?"

"Like?"

"Like the murder of Ryder Hayes's wife five years ago. Like the supposedly accidental deaths of two other rookies exactly one year apart. Like the death of my sister." He pinched the bridge of his nose. "She was only thirty-two, Ellen."

She reached out and laid a hand on his shoulder. He felt the warmth of her hand and knew she felt the hard muscle beneath her palm. But more, he read the sympathy in her eyes and knew she felt the pain coming from his heart. A pain he hadn't realized he needed to share. Most people hadn't liked his sister. Respected her way with the animals, yes. But as far as liking her as a person? No way. And he couldn't say he didn't understand it, but…she was his *sister*. "I know, Lee," she said softly. "And I know you're grieving her every day." She dropped her hand and cleared her throat. "And yes, I'm convinced there's a connection. We all think so, we just can't prove it. Yet."

He nodded to the cell phone she still held in her hand. "Are you back on duty so you can get back to working on making that happen?"

"You're full of questions, aren't you?" She nodded. "I am."

He breathed in and finally managed to ask the question he'd been working up to. "Then, are you up for dinner tonight?"

She blinked at him. "Dinner?"

"Why not? How about the Cactus Café?" She bit her lip and he sighed. "Not like a date, Ellen, just dinner."

A hint of red crept into her cheeks. "Sure, that sounds good."

"Great. Now let's get busy with these dogs. Want to play a game of fetch?"

Ellen had enjoyed spending the time with Lee and watching him work with the dogs. The training session had gone extremely well. Even the puppies were charmed by him and wanted to please him. She glanced at her watch. Now she had a meeting with an extraspecial client. She smiled. When she'd decided to put together the assistance program, she hadn't realized it would grow so big so quickly. Which was why she'd needed Lee and the other workers. She wondered if she'd really be able to leave when it came time. And she knew that time would come. She would have to make a choice. Stay or leave? The thought made her sad and antsy all at the same time. One things was certain, though. She was meant to be a cop. She just wasn't sure she could be one in the same town where mother lived. And ruled. She stepped into the lobby area of the training center and spotted her client at the same time the little girl saw her.

"Ms. Ellen! Ms. Ellen!"

Ellen grinned as Gabby Crenshaw rolled toward her in her motorized wheelchair. Gabby's mother, Patty, hur-

ried behind her, trying to keep up. The child had cere-
bral palsy so her words were slurred, but the smile on
her face had Ellen's heart singing. She waited for Gabby
to roll to a stop, then squatted next to the nine-year-old.
"Hello, Mrs. Crenshaw and little miss Gabby, how are
you two today?"

"I'm good." She waved her hand, then tried to clap as
she bounced in her seat. Her body might be twisted and
bent from the disorder and her movements awkward, but
her love of life was infectious. "I came to see Popcorn."

Ellen smoothed a hand down the child's messy ponytail and smiled up at Mrs. Crenshaw. The woman looked
harried and tired, but when she looked at her child, love
shone in her eyes. Ellen looked back at Gabby. "Then,
let's go find him. Do you remember where to go?"

"Yes ma'am!" Ellen stood, took Gabby's right hand
and let the child lead the way. She walked alongside
the humming chair and together they entered the kennel area. The training center was designed to be wheelchair accessible, but she'd paid special attention to this
area. Those clients who came to be trained to work with
their dogs had to learn to let them out of their temporary
homes and how to put them back in.

Gabby let out a low squeal of delight when she spotted her companion in his kennel. She looked up at Ellen.
"I missed him."

"I'm sure he missed you, too." Gabby wheeled over
to Popcorn's cage and released the lock. The black Lab
stepped out, his tail wagging. Popcorn was a gentle soul
who seemed to understand he had to contain some of his
energy when around the little girl. Gabby leaned forward
to wrap her arms around the Lab's neck and bury her

face against his fur. Popcorn simply stood there and let her. Ellen smiled. "Are you ready?"

"Ready." Gabby leaned back. "Come, Popcorn. Want a treat?"

The Lab's ears perked up and he followed Gabby to the treat jar. Gabby lifted the lid with slow, measured movements, used her other hand to scoop out some treats, then carefully replaced the lid. She dropped the treats into her lap, then turned to look at her mother and Ellen. "I did it!"

"You sure did," Ellen said. "Great job." She thought she caught a glint of tears in Patty's eyes. Her own throat tightened and she cleared it.

Gabby let out a chuckle and spun her chair around to face the door. Popcorn walked with her, his gaze on her, tongue lolling out of the side of his mouth.

Once in the training room, Ellen let Gabby take over while she looked around at the other children, service animals and adults.

When they noticed her, they waved and she stopped to speak to each one. By the time she was ready to go, Ellen knew Gabby and her mother and Popcorn were in good hands.

And she realized her own were sweating. She rubbed them together and pondered what she'd agreed to.

A date with Lee. No, not a date with Lee.

Dinner with Lee.

Which was probably a date.

She drew in a deep breath and hoped her heart would survive it.

Ellen looked in the mirror and sighed. Why was she so nervous? She'd eaten many dinners with Lee and he hadn't had this crazy effect on her before. At least not in the sense that she was so tense she practically had the shakes. She'd brought him home after work to get the Jeep, and he'd left with promises to clean up fast and get back to pick her up. She'd offered to just meet him at the café as it was only four blocks away from her, but he'd insisted on driving. For some reason, Ellen had given in and agreed. Now she wondered what in the world she'd been thinking.

Carly perched on the edge of the bed, watching. "What do you think, girl?" Ellen asked.

Carly tilted her head then lowered it to her paws.

Ellen scowled. "That's not an answer. That's just staying neutral." Carly's eyes closed and Ellen smiled. She really appreciated the animal's company. She walked over to scratch the dog's ears. "You get the night off, girl. Enjoy it."

Carly licked her hand.

Ellen picked her cell phone up from the bed where she'd tossed it and punched in the number for the hospital. After getting the same message about her mother's condition, she breathed a prayer that God would let her mother wake up. *Please, God, don't let her die with all of the issues we still have to resolve. As crazy as she can make me, I still love her.*

She inhaled slowly and walked down the steps into the foyer. She heard a car pull into the drive. *Lee.* Her heart thudded and her hands were instantly sweaty. She swiped them down her black pencil skirt and wished she'd worn the slacks instead. She straightened the collar of her royal blue shirt and fingered the gold earrings dangling from her lobes. She was too dressed up. Yep, she should have worn the slacks. Or jeans. Maybe she could just run upstairs and change.

Then it was too late. He knocked on the door and she had no more time to think about it. She twisted the knob and opened the door. Lee stood there dressed in khakis and a dark T-shirt layered under an open short-sleeved collared shirt along with loafers and a gentle smile on his handsome face. Memories invaded her, a longing for what they'd had in the past swamped her. No, she didn't want the teenage love they'd shared. She wanted something more, something richer, deeper. Just...more.

Oh, no. No, no, no. She wasn't going to go there. She wasn't. She couldn't. "Hi," she said before giving an inward wince at the breathless quality of that one word.

"Hi." He blinked. "Wow, you look amazing."

She swallowed. "Thanks. So do you."

"Are you ready?"

Was she? "Sure." Ellen stepped outside and gave a relieved sigh that the heat of the day had dissipated, leaving the night air cool and refreshing. She pulled the door shut behind her and let him lead her to the Jeep he'd left running. She climbed in. The Cactus Café was one of her favorite places to eat and she looked forward to visiting it tonight.

Ten minutes later, they walked inside and she followed Lee to a private booth in the back. Once they'd gotten their drinks and place their orders, he clasped his hands in front of him on the table. "So," she said. "I'd ask you how your day went, but I think I already know that." Her phone rang and she glanced at the screen with a sigh. "Do you mind? It's the chief."

"Of course not."

"Hi, Chief."

"I don't have anything earth shattering—just wanted to let you know that spot on the news about Freddie Parrish is working. Someone spotted him at a gas station just outside town. They called it in, but by the time a cruiser got there, he'd disappeared."

"Oh. Okay."

"We're having them run the segment again. Be ready for some action if we get some leads."

"Of course."

"Talk to you later."

She hung up and relayed the message to Lee.

"Everyone always said Freddie was headed for trouble," he said.

"They said that about you, too."

He gave her a small smile. "I know—and they were right. But then I met you."

She bit her lip as her heart thudded. "And that made a difference?"

"A big one." He cleared his throat. "Do you mind if we talk about something else for a few minutes?"

Slightly disappointed that he obviously wanted to change the subject, she took a sip of her tea. She wanted to explore what he meant by the difference she'd made in his life. Instead, she nodded. "All right, but if it's about Veronica's death, I don't know any more than what we've already talked about."

"No, it's not that."

She arched a brow. "Then, what?"

"I was curious as to how the Desert Valley Police Department was suddenly able to hire five rookies when they'd been talking about making cutbacks."

Ellen frowned and shrugged. "What about it?"

"I was getting groceries the other day and Chief Jones was talking to Louise Donaldson."

"Okay."

"I didn't mean to listen in, but I walked past as Louise said something about wanting to know if the mayor planned to use Marian's money to hire her replacement when she retires—or use it to keep the rookies she'd paid for."

Her lips tightened, then she blew out a slow breath. "Yes, and?"

"What that tells me is that it was your mother who funded the hiring of the five new rookies—you included—and their dogs."

She went still. "Yes. She did." It wasn't like it was a secret. She supposed it would be news to Lee, who'd only been back in town for two weeks.

"And you're all right with that?" he asked.

She paused before replying. "I didn't say that I was all right with it. I just said she did. She means well and has the money to do some good. Just like I have the money to run the assistance center and do some good while I'm here."

"Come on, Ellen. You know your mother has *always* had a hard time letting you go. What if she did this to keep you close to home?"

The waiter chose that moment to deliver the food. He placed it on the table. "Anything else you need?" he asked.

"No, thanks," Ellen said, and Lee shook his head.

For the next few minutes, they focused on the food. She finally looked up. "You really believe she would do that?"

He sighed. "We both know how your mother works."

She went silent for a brief moment then looked up and met his gaze. "Yes, the evidence of my mother's manipulative actions can be a bit overwhelming when you consider the past, but there's no way she'd use her money to buy me a position here in town." The very thought made her stomach turn. Or was it turning because she wasn't 100 percent sure her mother wouldn't do exactly that?

"She would do exactly that and you know it."

Lee's echo of her own thoughts disturbed her. Ellen tossed her napkin to the table next to her half-eaten dinner. "I'm not hungry anymore. I can see myself home, thanks."

He groaned and dropped his head. "Ellen—"

"This was a mistake. We can work together, but given your feelings about my mother—and the fact that you think I'm just like her—I don't see how we can… socialize. I'll see you tomorrow, Lee."

"So you're just going to walk out?"

She sighed. "No, I'm not just going to walk out. I'm finished. With the food and this conversation."

His eyes flashed. "Fine. I'll take you home."

"It's not necessary. It's four blocks up the street. I can walk." She tossed enough money on the table to cover her food and his. For the first time in her life, she was thankful her mother's house sat in the middle of town on Main Street. "I'll see you tomorrow."

"Ellen—"

"Tomorrow, Lee." She ignored the look of frustration on his face and headed for the door. Her mind spun. She was so tired of debating this with herself—and others who obviously thought the same thing. It wasn't the first time she'd been aware of the speculation regarding her mother's true motives in putting up the money, but it still got under her skin. Yes, there was the possibility that her mother had once again interfered in her life. In a huge way. Sure, she knew her mother had offered to pay the salaries of the rookies so they could get some answers and find Veronica's killer, but she hadn't done it specifically to keep Ellen in town.

Or had she? And that was the million-dollar question, wasn't it? Too bad her mother had been attacked before she had a chance to bring up the subject. She shouldn't have hesitated in asking. Then again, why did she even care? It wasn't as though it was a permanent assignment. The job would end and she would move on. Regardless of what her mother had or hadn't done. But it still irritated her.

Ellen walked home, the cool of the night a welcome respite from the heat that burned when the sun was up. She walked up the drive and glanced around. Her parents had been blessed with family money, and the large yellow house Ellen had grown up in was now on the historic register. Yes, blessed. So her mother had done something good with her money. That was fine, right? Great, even. But now, thanks to Lee, Ellen couldn't help wondering about the motivation behind the goodness.

She opened the front door and whistled to Carly. The dog bounded into the foyer and Ellen shut the front door behind her. "Come on, girl, you need to go out?"

Carly padded to the back door and Ellen opened it for her. While Carly sniffed bushes and took care of business, Ellen's brain whirled. She pulled her phone from her pocket and let her finger hover over Chief Jones's number. He was friends with her mother. He could answer the question once and for all about the woman's motives. No, she didn't want to bother him. She dialed Louise Donaldson's number. It's possible the deputy would know. She and the chief were friendly. The call went to voice mail. "Louise, when you get this message, will you give me a call? I have a question for you. Thanks." She hung up and called for Carly. "Come on, girl. Let's go check on our new friends. I'm restless and need something to do besides think." What she needed to do was apologize to Lee. She shouldn't have left that way. The way he'd left when he'd been mad at her for questioning his involvement with Freddie Parrish in prison. The same way her father had left her mother when he couldn't take it anymore.

The same way she'd left town so she wouldn't have to deal with her mother.

If everyone kept leaving, nothing would get resolved.

So she owed Lee an apology and the consideration of hearing him out. He was entitled to his opinion.

Carly trotted over and Ellen led the way to her SUV and opened the back door. Carly hopped in and made herself comfortable while Ellen slid into the driver's seat.

As she drove, her mother stayed at the forefront of her spinning thoughts. Would she have truly handed over that much money, been so manipulative, just to make sure Ellen returned—and stayed in—Desert Valley? Now that Lee had brought it up again, she couldn't stop the question from looping through her mind. She had to know. One way or another. Then again, would knowing for sure make any difference? Maybe. Maybe not. She wouldn't know until she *knew*. She glanced at her phone, hoping Louise would call her back tonight.

She arrived at the training center and let Carly out of the car. The dog trotted to the front door of the assistance center and Ellen went to unlock it but found the door cracked open. "What?"

She pulled her weapon and gave the door a gentle push. It swung in on silent hinges. She stepped inside, Carly at her side. The dog was tense and alert. "Hello?" Where was the night security guard? After all the recent trouble at the training center, she'd hired two men to rotate watching the place at night. They'd started two weeks ago and, thankfully, had reported no problems. So where was he?

"Benny? Frank?" She wasn't sure who was on duty tonight but she saw no sign of either of them. Carly nosed her way to the back where the kennels were and Ellen gasped. The kennel doors had been opened. The pups were trapped in the larger open area and were playing with one another. But it wasn't the pups that had captured her attention, it was the body sprawled in front of the cages that swept the breath from her lungs. "Benny!"

She started forward, heard the footsteps behind her and Carly's low growl. She turned to see a figure dressed in black lifting a gun to aim it in her direction. Ellen's training rose to the surface and she lashed out with her right foot and slammed her heel into his arm. The gun spun from his hand and skidded across the floor and under a chair. He cursed and dived at her. Carly barked and lunged, throwing herself against the intruder's back. He landed hard on the floor then scrambled to his feet. But Ellen was already moving, and she threw a solid punch into his face. He screamed and reared back against the reception desk. Ellen's fist throbbed, but she went for her weapon just as something crashed into the side of her head. More pain flashed, Carly barked and Ellen tumbled to the floor.

FIVE

Lee sighed and pushed a hand through his hair. Why hadn't he just kept his mouth shut? He sat in the borrowed Jeep across the street from Ellen's home and wondered where she'd gone. Not fifteen minutes after she'd walked out of the café, he'd driven over to apologize, and now she wasn't answering her door. He frowned and glanced at the clock on the dash. He'd give her a few more minutes. Maybe she'd stopped in at one of the stores along Main Street. An idea hit him. He climbed from the Jeep and walked to the garage. A quick glance in the window revealed her car was gone. So. She'd come home, gotten her car and left again.

He got back in the Jeep and pondered what to do. He really didn't want to go home with the tension still between them. Could she have gotten a call from the hospital about her mother?

Possibly. He dialed the number to the hospital. "Hi, I'd like to check on Marian Foxcroft. Has there been any change in her condition?"

"Are you a family member?"

"No, a family friend." Sort of.

"Then, I can't give out that information."

He sighed. "Okay, could you at least tell me if her daughter, Ellen, is there with her?"

"Hold just a moment, please." He held. In seconds she came back on the line. "She's not here."

"All right. Thanks."

He hung up. So where would she go? She could have gotten a call about the case she was working, but most likely, workaholic that he knew her to be, she'd gone to the kennels. She'd been mad when she'd left the restaurant. Even in high school when she'd been upset she'd gone to find an animal to love on.

The puppies would make her feel better. He aimed his car in the direction of the kennel and again considered the fact that Marian had paid for the rookies to be assigned to Desert Valley. He knew Ellen didn't want to believe Marian had done it to force Ellen to stay in town after graduating from the K-9 center, but Lee knew he was right.

He also knew Ellen would want to find out immediately if that was true, and he hoped she got her answers before the question drove her nuts.

Ellen lay on the floor, her head pounding. She hadn't blacked out, but the hit had stunned her. She rolled to see the figure grabbing at the puppies. He snagged one. She reached for her weapon and found it wedged under her right hip. Relief swept through her. She wrapped her fingers around it and brought it up. Now he was going after the one of the other pups.

She brought the gun up. "Police! Freeze or I'll shoot!"

He spun, the one puppy he had a hold on wriggled from his grasp and fell to the floor. His weapon followed. Her vision blurred and she hoped she'd be able to hit him if she had to pull the trigger. A curse slipped from his lips and he started toward the gun.

"Touch it and I'll shoot you!" she shouted.

He froze and backed toward the door.

She tracked him with her weapon. "Don't move." The words echoed in her skull as did the pain that came with shouting them.

He cast one more glance at the gun on the floor. "I'll be back," he whispered as he slipped out the door. She tried to scramble to her feet, but the room swam. She gritted her teeth and shut her eyes. She had to let him go.

Something wet swiped her face and she gasped. Then blinked against the assault of the puppy's tongue on her cheek. She lifted a hand to her head with a groan and swallowed a wave of nausea as she squinted through still-blurry eyes.

Wait a minute. She slowly turned her head. And there was Benny, quiet and still on the floor next to her. "Benny," she whispered. She moved toward him, ignoring the pain racing through her head. She slipped her fingers over his wrist and bit her lip on a cry of relief. A pulse. A strong one.

Her phone. Where was it?

She slapped a hand against her waist and found the device still in the clip. With a grimace and a groan, fighting dizziness and the desire to black out, she unclipped it and hit the second speed-dial button on the screen. She knew Ryder was on duty tonight, so she tried his personal number first. And he answered.

"Ryder?"

"Yeah? Ellen? You okay?"

"I need backup at the training center. And an ambulance."

"Are you hurt?"

She could hear him scrambling in the background. "I'm all right, but Benny, the security guard, was attacked, too. He's still unconscious."

"Tristan and I were having a late dinner, discussing Veronica's murder. He and I are about three minutes away. We're moving now."

"Okay."

"Is the attacker still in the building?"

"No. He left. Unfortunately, I couldn't stop him." At least the one she had seen had left. What if he'd had a partner? Partner... Carly. Where was Carly? Fear for the animal hit her. "Carly?"

Through the phone she heard a car door slam and knew her fellow officers were on the way. "Where's Carly?" Tristan demanded. She must be on speaker-phone.

"I don't know. I remember hearing her bark and then I was hit on the head."

"Hit on the head!" Ryder yelled. "I thought you said you weren't hurt."

"I said I was all right. And I am."

"You still have your weapon?"

"Yes. I fell on it when I was knocked out. I have a feeling Carly and I surprised the intruder and the only thing on his mind was getting away." But what if there was someone else there? There'd been two people in the vehicle when she and Lee had been attacked on the way back from the prison. And only one had left the center. She got to her feet and swayed. She held her weapon in her right hand and braced herself against the nearest kennel fence. Where was Carly? She didn't want to call out again. Not yet. Not until she knew if anyone else was in the building.

When her head quit spinning, she listened to the puppies yapping and playing, but she tried to hear beyond them. She heard nothing, but that didn't mean anything. What did they want? He'd gone after the dogs. But why? Her head still throbbed but her mind was clearing along with her eyes.

She heard Ryder calling to her and realized when she'd braced herself against the chain-link fence, she'd lowered the phone from her ear. She pressed it back to her ear. "Hey, I'm still here. I think whoever broke in left, and I don't think anyone else was with him."

"Stay put. Don't go looking for anyone else."

She realized she didn't have the strength to go after anyone. She leaned her back against the cage and let her legs fold her back to the floor. "I'm not looking. Trust me. I'm just going to be sitting here." But she wanted to find Carly. Sirens sounded and drew closer quickly. "I think I hear the ambulance."

"We're pulling in, too."

Just one of the perks of living in a small town. Help was never too far away. Ellen took a deep breath and moved back to the fallen security officer. That was when she noticed the glass bowl on the tile floor. Strands of long light brown hair were stuck to the drying blood. Her hair. So that was what he'd hit her with.

She checked Benny's pulse once more and squeezed his hand. "Help is on the way, Benny, hang on."

Lee pulled into the parking lot of the training center and leaped out of his car. Flashing blue-and-red lights shouted trouble. "Ellen!" He spotted her SUV in the first parking spot next to the door and rushed toward the entrance.

"Hey, you can't go in there."

Lee realized it was Chief Jones himself who had the iron grip on his forearm. "I have to see if Ellen's all right."

"She's fine. She's giving a statement right now."

Lee felt his pulse slow slightly. The chief released him. "Good. What happened?"

"Someone broke in."

Lee resisted rolling his eyes. "I figured that. And the alarm didn't go off?"

"Benny, the night security guard Ellen hired when she started the training center, was caught by surprise."

"Is he all right?"

"Yes. He was out cold for a while but was waking up by the time the ambulance arrived. I was able to talk to him a bit before they pushed me away to check on him."

"So what did he say?"

"Someone knocked on the door. Benny said when he looked out, he saw a person standing there with his back to him. He had a large dog in his arms. Thinking it was someone who wanted to drop off a stray animal, Benny immediately disabled the alarm and opened the door. When he did, the masked person dropped the dog, spun and jammed a gun into Benny's stomach. Benny backpedaled and the attacker shoved him off balance then cracked the gun on his head. Twice."

"Ouch."

"Exactly. And he got Ellen with a heavy bowl that had dog treats in it."

"I thought you said she was all right." He started toward the door and once again the chief stopped him.

"She'll probably have a headache, but she's fine."

Lee ran a hand through his hair. What was going on in this town? Would it never end? "Did you get a description from Benny?"

"No, the mask kind of prevented that."

Lee refused to grit his teeth with the frustration running rampant through him. "Of course. I meant like height, weight, details like that."

"Not yet. We'll ask those questions soon. He's off to the hospital for now to get a head X-ray."

"Lee?"

Lee turned at the sound of Ellen's voice. "Hey." He noticed her gloved hand holding something against the side of her head. An ice pack. The other gloved hand held a crystal bowl he remembered seeing the treats in. "How bad are you hurt?"

"He stunned me for a few seconds." She grimaced. "Long enough to get away."

"You should be in the hospital."

"No way." She looked back. "Carly, heel." Carly appeared at her side. "We're going to see what we can find." She handed Lee the ice pack and held the bowl in a gloved hand to let Carly sniff it. "Track, Carly." Carly immediately went to work, her nose to the ground. Ellen set the bowl on the ground and motioned to an officer. "Bag that, will you?"

Without waiting for an answer, Ellen followed behind Carly. Lee stayed with them. Carly bypassed the law enforcement and went in almost a straight line all the way to the edge of the road where she sat with a whine. Ellen knelt beside the dog and scratched her ears. "This is where the getaway car was, I guess. She's lost the scent." Ellen stood and winced, her hand pressing to her head for a brief moment. Then she slipped Carly a chew toy and the dog latched on to it. Her reward for doing a good job.

"Ellen, you need to get that looked at."

"I've got a pretty hard head. Want to come help me get the puppies put away for the remainder of the night?"

"Well, if you're not going to take care of yourself…"

"I'm taking care of myself. It wasn't that hard of a hit."

"Fine." Lee followed her and Carly away from the road and back into the building, where he noticed the deputies gathering evidence and going over what was now a crime scene. He hoped they knew what they were doing. As far as he could tell, Ryder Hayes and Chief Jones were the only really competent officers on the force—discounting the other rookies. He shook his head and gathered the pups. And Chief Jones was counting his days.

"I had the new puppies in the back area of the kennel," Ellen said. "I wanted them away from the other dogs so they wouldn't pick up any bad habits." Carly came to her side and sat. She placed a hand on the dog's head. "Whoever did this managed to get Carly in one of the kennels and lock her in. I found her just before I took her out to track."

"She didn't fight back?"

"No. Once the person wasn't attacking me anymore, she stood down. And that worries me."

He nodded. "Because it means it's someone she knows and likely trusts."

"Possibly—or it could simply mean the person who did this is comfortable around dogs and knows how to be the alpha."

"That's just awesome." He glanced around and noticed something that interested him. "Tristan and Ryder seem to be leading this. Chief Jones is just kind of standing back."

Ellen sighed. "Chief Jones is ready to retire. He's good at his job, but he's already made it known that he has one foot out the door and he's not worried about letting the up-and-coming officers take over a bit."

"Yes, that's what I'm hearing. I have a feeling he'll retire before much longer."

Ellen rubbed her eyes. "Okay, so I'm going to get this place cleaned up, see if the video footage got anything and then head home for some sleep."

"All right, let's get it done."

"Thanks." She started to turn and he gently clasped her upper arm. She looked at him.

"I'm sorry," he said.

She bit her lip and gave a short nod. "Thank you, but I've been thinking about what you said and you're right. I do know how my mother operates. I can't say I haven't thought about it, but I want to know for sure if she had ulterior motives behind her more than generous offer. I've got a call in to Louise Donaldson to ask her about it, but—" Her eyes locked on Chief Jones who was standing by his cruiser. "I guess I can find out right now."

"Ellen, it doesn't matter."

"Yes. Yes, it does."

SIX

Ellen stepped up next to Chief Jones, who was talking to Ryder and Tristan, whose dogs sat at their sides, alert and ready for action should they be called to it. Tristan's yellow Lab, Jesse, looked over at Ellen's approach. Ryder's dog, Titus, simply tilted his head.

"...called about the glove. They didn't find any prints, but they got some DNA off it."

"They're running it through CODIS?" Ryder asked.

"They are."

The men looked at her, as well. "How are you feeling?" Chief Jones asked.

"I had some ibuprofen and took a couple. I'll be okay. It was a hard knock, but I don't have a concussion, according to the paramedic."

"Good to hear," Chief Jones said. "You need some time off?"

"No." He lifted a brow and she shrugged. "If something changes between now and tomorrow I'll let you know. I've had worse headaches than this. Really, it was just a glancing blow." She cleared her throat. "Are you talking about the bank robbery?"

"Yes."

"So they found DNA on the glove. That's great."

"Yes, I'd love to have this case solved and soon."

"There are a lot of cases that need solving and soon," Lee muttered.

The chief looked at him. "Yes, we're concentrating on that one, too, Lee."

Tristan nodded to Ellen. "You need to take care of yourself," he said. "Head injuries aren't anything to play around with."

"And I will. But for now, Chief, I want to ask you a question and I want a straight answer."

The chief frowned at her. "Of course."

"I've heard a lot of speculation about my mother's motives in putting up the money to pay for the rookies' salaries and I'm tired of wondering about it. You're friends with her. Did she have an ulterior motive?"

"Like?"

"Like forcing me to come home so she could have me under her thumb again."

His deer-in-headlights look gave her the answer she didn't want. Her shoulders slumped and she felt Lee's hand at the small of her back. Her head throbbed harder and she swallowed. Well, she'd wanted to know and now she did.

"Come here." He took her arm and pulled her aside. She felt Ryder's, Lee's and Tristan's gazes follow them. "Ellen, it doesn't matter how we got you here. You're here to do a job that needs to be done and that's all that matters."

Her fingers curled into fists at her side. "But she once again has interfered in my life. Lee was right. She did it because she wanted me home."

He sighed and shifted his heavy belt. "I'm not going

to say that your staying in Desert Valley had nothing to do with her offer. Your mother loves you. But mostly she wanted the murders of Melanie Hayes, Mike Riverton and Brian Miller solved. She said their deaths were a pall over the town and she wanted it gone. She started ranting about how Desert Valley was losing residents and tourist dollars and how her ancestors who founded the town would be so disappointed."

Ellen refrained from rolling her eyes. Barely. "Ah, yes, the ancestors." Hadn't she heard enough about them and living up to their expectations her entire life?

The chief cleared his throat and continued. "She was also mad because the county fair last year only brought in about half of its normal visitors. Said something had to be done and it looked like it was up to her to do it."

"Unbelievable," Ellen muttered.

"I know it sounds manipulative and maybe part of it had to do with getting you home, but truly, I think she was more concerned about the town losing revenue than keeping you here."

She didn't believe it for a moment. "Nice try, Chief, but you can't cover for her, and I can't ask her myself. If you know her motives, come clean, will you, please?"

He sighed. "Ellen, come on. I'm not covering for her. The morning after Veronica was killed, Marian showed up with her offer. She said if we would hire you five rookies who had just graduated Veronica's class, then she would bestow the training center with a half-million-dollar endowment and pay the rookies' salaries for as long as it took to solve the murders. Since you all hadn't been assigned anywhere at the time she made the offer, the governor thought it sounded like a win-win situation." He cleared his throat. "And honestly, I can't say I wasn't relieved to have the help."

"I see."

"Would she have done it if you hadn't been one of the rookies hired?" He shrugged. "I don't know. I don't really care to be honest. I'm just glad y'all are here."

Ellen's throat worked. She didn't know whether she wanted to scream or stomp her feet.

Or both.

Both.

Definitely both.

She drew in a calming breath. "All right, then. Let's focus on solving this case as fast as possible." Because only then would she be free to leave Desert Valley—and her mother—for good. Assuming her mother ever woke up. The twinge of grief that pierced her at the thought of her mother never waking didn't catch her by surprise this time. She loved her mother, she just didn't want to live in the same town with her. And she sure didn't want to be around so the woman could hone her manipulation skills on her.

Ellen pushed the grief away and told herself not to go there. She waved Lee over. Tristan and Ryder followed. "Have you found anything that might lead us to the person responsible for this latest incident?" Ellen asked.

"Well, the only thing left behind that might tell us anything was the bowl that was used to hit you. We'll check for prints."

"Don't bother. He wore gloves." She remembered turning, the flash of the gloved hand, the crashing pain against her head.

"And it's likely someone who's familiar enough with

the program to know that the door would be opened to anyone with a pet in his arms," Lee said.

Ellen nodded, then grimaced. "And that."

"Come on, I'm taking you to the hospital to get your head looked at," Lee said.

She waved a dismissing hand. "The paramedic already checked me out."

"Yeah, well, I want a doctor giving you the green light."

"I'd feel better about that, too," Chief Jones said. "Go with him."

"Come on, Chief, it's a twenty-minute drive out there and back."

"Go see your mother while you're there. Give her my best."

Ellen stilled. She knew when she was outnumbered—and knew an order when she heard one. And the mention of seeing her mother again was compelling. "Fine."

Lee pulled the keys to her mother's Jeep from his pocket. "Chief, can you lock up here?"

"Of course. Tristan, why don't you follow them? Watch their backs. After the shooting and now this, I'm afraid we're all going to need to have each others' backs."

Tristan nodded. "I can do that."

Lee shot Ellen a smug look. "There you go. No more excuses. Everything's taken care of."

She groaned, not really upset about going, but not wanting to be bossed around, either. A smile played at the corner of Lee's mouth. He knew exactly what she was thinking. She commanded Carly to heel and followed him to the vehicle. Carly took the backseat and Ellen climbed into the passenger seat. Once Lee was settled behind the wheel and they were pulling away from the parking lot of the training center, she looked at him. And kept her mouth shut. She let him drive while she thought. The minutes passed quickly and the silence stretched.

"I don't think you're like her," he finally said.

"What?"

"I don't really think you're like your mother. I shouldn't have said that you were."

"Oh. Thanks. I'm glad."

He sighed.

"What are you thinking?" he asked.

She touched the wound on her head and winced. "About this break-in."

"Of course. What about it?"

She glanced at him. "I keep circling back to the fact that it's similar to the others."

"The others?"

"The ones I was telling you about. Where someone breaks in to a house or whatever, but doesn't take anything."

"Right, you mentioned that. So they're looking for something."

"Yes."

"The German shepherd puppy that's missing?"

"Yeah. Marco. All of the break-ins are the same, including this one. It's the only thing that makes sense. There's a lot of equipment in that building that's worth a lot of money, and yet nothing was taken." She sighed and closed her eyes, wishing she could just put all the pieces together and get this thing solved.

"Maybe they didn't have time? Maybe you got there before they had a chance."

"Maybe, but I'm guessing the training center was just next on the list of places to hit to look for Marco."

"Where do you think they'll go next?" he asked.

"I don't know." She sat up, her mind spinning as much as it could with the pounding in her skull. "But that's a really good question."

"What do you mean?"

"We can get a map, make a list of all the places already hit and narrow it down to a few possibilities that could be next." She had her phone out and was punching in a group text to Ryder, Shane, Whitney James and Tristan.

When she finished, her phone pinged several times. Great idea. We're on it, Ryder texted back.

She gave him a half smile. "Nice job."

"Glad I can be helpful." He paused and turned right.

"Why do they want that puppy, Marco, so bad?" she whispered. "What is so special about that dog that someone would go to such lengths to find him?"

"All of the puppies are worth a lot of money," Lee said. "They're purebred."

"I know that. But I just have a feeling there's something more going on with that puppy than we're seeing."

He parked and turned the Jeep off. "Well, we'll have to discuss it later. We're here."

At Canyon County Medical Center, the doctor reiterated the paramedic's diagnosis of no concussion but said that she needed rest.

Tristan had come in to wait, as well. Even Shane had shown up. The two officers and Lee had discussed the case while Ellen had her head examined. When she came out of the room, Lee took in her pinched features and tired eyes. "Take the day off tomorrow and take it easy," he said. Then wondered why he bothered. He was probably just wasting his breath.

"I may try to sleep in, but no promises after that."

Shane raised a brow. Tristan met Lee's gaze and Lee sighed. "Well, one thing worked in your favor tonight," he said.

"What's that?"

"Your hard head."

Tristan and Shane snickered, and Ellen wrinkled her nose at Lee. "Funny."

"Hey, you took a hard knock and didn't get a concussion. The evidence speaks for itself."

She gave him a light punch on the arm.

"Okay, heads up," Tristan said. "I've got news."

Ellen turned serious. "What?"

"Ryder's mapped all the break-ins and pinpointed two other homes that are possible targets. They're families that recently got German shepherd puppies but haven't been broken into yet. We thought we'd set a trap and see if we can catch whoever's doing this."

"What kind of trap?"

"It'll take some coordination, but I think we can pull it off. We'll have two teams. We'll ask one of the families to leave for the evening and not come home until we give them the okay. We'll have them make it well-known that they won't be at home and hopefully word will filter down to the person we're after."

Ellen nodded. "I see where you're going with this."

"Have the break-ins happened on a specific night of the week?" Lee asked.

Tristan shook his head. "Not that we can see. A couple of Mondays, a weekend, several Thursdays."

"But none of the owners were home," Shane said,

looking at his phone. "I've got the reports here. All of the break-ins were when the home owners were gone."

Tristan scratched his chin. "Yes, that's one of the common denominators."

"Tell me about the two remaining families who have German shepherd puppies and no break-in," Ellen said.

"One is an elderly homebound resident."

"And the other?"

"Works here at the hospital third shift, but her husband and kids are home at night while she's working."

"And she'd be sleeping during the day while the husband works and the kids are at school," Ellen said.

"But it's only a matter of time before one of the houses is empty. The weekend is coming up. The multishift family will spend the day at the lake or the elderly resident will have a doctor's appointment. Something."

"And that's when our would-be puppy snatcher will strike."

"Exactly. That's why we're going to give this person the perfect opportunity. An empty house and a German shepherd puppy," Tristan said.

Shane nodded. "Let's get it set up." He stifled a yawn.

Ellen did the same. "I know we're all tired, but before we leave I need to check on my mother. I can't come here and not go see her. Do you three mind?"

"I don't mind," Shane said. "If Tristan has this, I'm going to head into the office for a bit and work on this plan of ours."

Tristan nodded. "I got it."

Ellen looked at Lee. "Are you sure you don't mind?"

"Of course you have to see her," Lee said. "Lead the way."

Shane took off for the sliding glass doors while Ellen

headed for the elevators with Carly at her side. Lee, Tristan and his Lab, Jesse, stepped in beside her. They made their way to the fourth floor and Ellen led them to the nurse's station. Lee noted the looks Tristan and Jesse got as well as Ellen and Carly. People wanted to pet the dogs, but the official working-dog vests they wore were sufficient to keep most people at bay. "You can wait here," Ellen said. "I'll be right back. Her room is the second one on the left." She told Carly to stay with Lee and headed in that direction.

Lee scratched the dog's ears and watched Ellen speak to the guard sitting outside the door. She nodded then slipped into the room. The floor was quiet, the atmosphere subdued. Tristan pulled his phone from his pocket. "Excuse me while I make a call? I need to check on my sister." Jesse stayed right at his side watching Tristan's every move.

"Sure."

Tristan walked a few paces away and pressed the phone to his ear. Lee checked his own phone, but no one had called or texted. Sadness invaded him. He and Veronica hadn't been close. Not like some siblings, but at least he'd known she was there if he needed her. Only someone had taken that away from him, and it angered him. The injustice of it, the personal loss, everything.

Ellen appeared in the doorway. She stopped, spoke to the guard again, then swiped at her eyes and took a deep breath. She looked up and caught his gaze on her and offered him a shaky smile as she walked toward him. "Thanks for waiting."

"No problem. Are you okay?"

"I am. It just hurts to see her so incapacitated. I mean, we've had our moments, arguments and disagreements, for sure. Definitely plenty of those. But I always knew she was there for me if I truly needed her to be, you know what I mean?"

Exactly what he'd just been thinking about Veronica. Lee's throat clogged with a sudden tightness. He cleared it. "I'm sorry," he said.

"I am, too."

"No, I mean I'm sorry about…before."

Her brow knit. "Before?"

"In high school." He sighed and ran a hand through his hair. "We were so young and I was…stupid. I thought if you truly loved me you should choose me over your mother. That…I don't know…that we'd run away together and live happily ever after."

She bit her lip and looked away. "I know."

"I was wrong and I'm sorry. I shouldn't have put that burden on you. Given you that ultimatum."

"No. But like you said, we were young. And stupid. I have to take some of the credit, too."

He gave her a small smile and rested a hand on her upper arm. "I've missed you, Ellen."

She nodded. "I've missed you, too, Lee, and I just want you—"

"Are you two ready?"

Lee turned to see Tristan and Jesse standing behind him. Frustration bit at him. What had she been about to say? He smoothed his features. "We're ready. Ellen?"

She shot him a quiet look full of regret then shrugged. "I'm ready. Take me to get my car, so I can go home and get that rest you keep harping about."

"I have the right to harp," Lee said. "A doctor backed me up."

She gave a low chuckle. "I'm not going to win tonight, am I?"

"No."

"Fine." She and Carly followed him out of the hospital and to the Jeep while Tristan and Jesse jogged to Tristan's vehicle and climbed in. Once she had the door shut and her seat belt on, she laid her head back and closed her eyes.

Lee smiled and pulled out of the hospital parking lot. He'd take her to get her car and then get some rest himself. He had a feeling tomorrow was going to be a long day. As he drove, he watched the road behind him. Every time he passed a side road, he tensed, almost expecting someone to dart out in front of him.

The fact that he knew Tristan was on guard behind him offered him a large measure of comfort. Apparently it worked for Ellen, too, as within seconds her breathing turned deep and even. Good. She needed to sleep. He drove slower than he needed to, stretching out the minutes to give her as much rest as he could before pulling into the parking lot of the training center. With regret that he couldn't give her more time to sleep, he nudged her. "We're here."

She opened her eyes and blinked at him. "Did I fall asleep?"

"Naw, you were just resting your eyes while you thought about the case."

She laughed and yawned. "Right. We'll go with that one." She studied him for a moment then leaned over and placed a kiss on his cheek. "Thanks, Lee."

Surprise held him still. Surprise and emotions he'd thought—hoped—he'd buried long ago. He lifted a hand, slid it under her loose ponytail and gently grasped the back of her neck. Her eyes widened and she opened her mouth as though to say something, then closed it and swallowed hard. He leaned in, never taking his eyes from hers. Closer. His gaze dropped to her lips and she tensed. He paused. Then dropped his hand and leaned back. "Good night, Ellen."

She let out a little puff of breath that whispered across his cheek. Tristan's headlight flashed through the interior of the Jeep. Ellen stared at him a moment longer, and he would have given anything to know what she was thinking behind the intense gaze. "Good night, Lee. Drive safe."

She climbed out and shut the door, then opened the back so Carly could jump out. He watched her and Carly walk to her car. Ellen looked back. This time there was no problem reading the expression on her face. Longing with a hint of fear. Not a fear for her physical safety but for her emotional well-being. He let his lips curve. Good. He wanted her off balance. Because he planned to finish what they'd started in high school. He planned to make it his mission to convince her that they belonged together. The timing had been wrong when they were teens. Their time was now.

As soon as Veronica's murderer was caught.

Or before, if it came down to it.

He wanted justice for his sister. He craved it, wanted to demand it and have it happen. But he knew there was the distinct possibility that whoever had killed Veronica might actually get away with it. The thought made him want to shout out a huge denial, but he stayed silent and watched Ellen drive away. He knew she and the team were working on the case—cases, if one included the other deaths—and he also knew that they didn't have a whole lot to work with. *God, don't let whoever did this get away with it. Please.*

Tristan waited patiently in his vehicle with Jesse in the backseat. Lee walked over. "I'm just going to check on the puppies." He noticed the police cruiser in the parking lot. "Who's that?"

"The chief asked Eddie Harmon to stay the rest of the night to keep an eye on the center."

Eddie? Lee kept his groan to himself. Eddie wouldn't notice if a crook came up and slapped him in the face with a handwritten confession. He was a good man but a lousy cop. "Ah…okay. I'm sure his wife is going to love that. I'll be right back." Everyone knew Eddie was more of a family man than a cop. He'd rather be carrying a baby on his hip than a gun.

"I'll wait," Tristan said. "I'll escort you home when you're ready. Ellen and the chief have arranged for an officer to keep an eye on your place tonight, too."

"Who?"

"Dennis Marlton."

"Okay." Dennis was in his early sixties and retiring this year. Having him watching his home didn't inspire much confidence. So Eddie was on the center and Dennis was on Lee's home. Great. He'd be sure to sleep with one eye open.

As though his thoughts had transmitted to Tristan, the man smiled. "Dennis is older, I know, but hopefully having him sitting in his official vehicle will deter anyone who might come snooping around."

What choice did he have? "That's fine. Sit tight, I won't be long."

He made his way into the building and to the puppies in their kennel at the front. They yipped when they saw him, and he gave them each a scratch and a treat. They were fine. He could go home and rest easy. If he could shut his mind off, that was. He slipped back out the door and made sure it was locked tight with the alarm set. He started the engine and waved to Tristan, who followed at a safe distance.

The training center was only about a five-minute drive from his home, and when he pulled into the long drive he saw the cruiser sitting off to the side. The officer waved and Lee kept going. He was glad to be home, glad that Ellen was safe. And doubly glad Ellen had turned at the last moment so he got a glimpse of her inner feelings.

Because there were two things he knew with rock-solid certainty. He wanted to finish veterinarian school and open his own practice. And number two, he wanted to be in Ellen's life on a permanent basis. He just had to convince her that she wanted that, too. He could do that.

"Right?" he whispered. He nodded. "Right. Maybe."

SEVEN

Ellen tossed and turned and finally threw the covers off and slid out of her bed. Carly lifted her head, and with the moon filtering through her blinds, Ellen could see the animal's annoyance with her. "Glad one of us can sleep."

Carly huffed and lowered her head back to her paws and shut her eyes. Ellen rubbed the dog's silky ears and then made her way down the hall and into the kitchen. She had to work tomorrow. She glanced at the clock. Today.

And she had to stop by the training center and leave some notes for those who would be working with the special-needs children and their dogs. Working on training and pairing animals to the appropriate child was a delicate dance but it was also one of her favorite things about working with the children. Seeing their eyes light up and watching them learn right along with their dog.

She yawned and hoped she wouldn't be worthless with her less-than-stellar night's sleep. She sighed and finally realized she needed to face the real reason she was restless. She could try to blame it on the unsolved murders. She could try to blame it on her still-throbbing head. The truth of the matter was that she was still re-playing the almost kiss.

Lee had come so close to kissing her, and she'd had a moment of indecision that he'd read as though it had been stamped on her forehead. And like the gentleman that he was—and had always been—he'd backed off.

Much to her regret now. No, she wouldn't regret it. There was no sense in getting her heart tangled up in his once again. She was his boss. She was leaving Desert Valley as soon as the opportunity presented itself. Kissing Lee would just make things much more complicated than they needed to be.

She groaned. "God, I don't know what's going on or where all this is leading, but I need Your guidance on it." She whispered the prayer aloud and it did seem to help calm her racing thoughts. "What's the right thing to do, God? You've brought me back to Desert Valley for a reason. Maybe my mother's sole purpose in giving the money to the police was to get me back here for an extended period time, so she'd have the opportunity to dictate my life again. I don't know. I don't know much of anything right now, since You've also brought Lee back into my life. Show me what I'm supposed to do with my feelings for him, okay?"

She paced back and forth, waiting to see if she had a sudden burst of inspiration. Nothing.

She sighed. Okay, so she didn't have a clear answer but she felt better taking the matter to the one who was in control. "Well, I'll just wait on Your timing, then. Okay, Lord?"

She went back into the bedroom and thought about Veronica's murder.

She'd been sprawled at the gate of the puppy yard

of the Canyon County Training Center and she'd been shot in the chest twice. The plan had been for her to microchip the puppies, then go over to James Harrison's home to give him a training refresher for his dog. Only she'd never made it over there. Who was responsible for her death and why was it taking so long to figure it out?

Ellen sighed and rubbed her eyes. Carly moved beside her and laid her head in Ellen's lap. Ellen scratched the dog's ears and let her eyes droop shut.

Lee gave up on sleep and sat on the edge of his bed while he thought. He was hot and it was stuffy in his room. He hated to turn the air on when the nights were cool. He walked to the window and lifted it a fraction, then padded down the hall to the kitchen. He grabbed a bottle of water from the refrigerator, then returned to his room and flopped on the bed again.

So. Ellen. He sighed. He'd almost kissed her. But then he'd come to his senses. She was his boss and he had to respect that. For now.

A sound from outside caught his attention and he sat up listening. Voices?

"...not in the house," the voice whispered.

Lee slid from the bed once again and moved on silent feet to the window while his heart pounded out a faster beat. Who wasn't in the house? Did they think he wasn't there? But the Jeep was right outside in plain sight.

"Keep looking." A lower voice. Deeper than the first. A voice he thought he recognized, but couldn't place. His adrenaline pumped. They were looking for something. What?

Lee moved to his end table and grabbed his phone from the charger. He hesitated only a fraction of a second before shooting a text to Ellen. A text she might not get. His backup plan had him punching in Officer Marlton's number. No answer. Where was the man? He dialed 911.

"Nine-one-one. Where is your emergency?"

He stepped into the hall, away from the open window, and gave her his address. "This is Lee Earnshaw. I have two people outside who are trespassing. I have an officer watching my home, but can't reach him."

"Who's the officer?"

"Dennis Marlton."

"Are the two men armed?"

"I don't know, but I'd assume they are."

"Stay hidden. Don't confront them. I have a unit on the way."

"Good."

"And stay on the line with me."

"Okay." He moved back into his bedroom and looked around for something he could use as a weapon. He didn't own a gun. Veronica had sold them all after he'd gone to prison. Might be time to buy another. There wasn't anything in his room he could see that would be a good defense against a gun. So he just wouldn't let them see him. But he'd try to figure out who they were and why there were there. He stood as close to the side of the window as he dared and looked out. The two men were still there, heads tilted toward one another and still talking in hushed tones. Lee leaned closer, but could only make out a few words.

"…the message…"

"…the backyard…"

"…boss is going to go ballistic if he doesn't get the information."

Information? About what? And why would he think Lee had it?

The two men headed for his backyard and he caught one more partial sentence. "…can't get the info without the dogs."

"Lee? Are you there?" The 911 dispatcher.

"Yes," he whispered when he figured it was safe. The two men had moved far enough away that they wouldn't hear him.

Something nagged at him. He hadn't gotten a good look at either of the two men, but there was something familiar about one of the voices.

"…they're not here, I'm telling you."

He sucked in a breath. They were back beneath the window. "Then, let's break in and beat the information out of him."

Lee heard that clear enough.

Where were the cops? He huddled near the window, listening to the sound of their footsteps heading toward his front door.

He grabbed a lamp from the end table next to his bed and carried it down the hall and into his foyer. He stood off to the side of the front door, his heart pounding. He'd had to defend himself enough times in prison that he knew he could handle himself if he had to. He'd learned how to move fast and fight dirty. Skills he hadn't planned on needing once he was out, but he might be glad he had them tonight.

The doorknob gave a light rattle, but he knew that unless they had a battering ram, they weren't getting in this way. The dead bolt was engaged; the knob lock was twisted into the locked position. Double protection that would keep them out. Would they dare break a window?

He didn't have an elaborate alarm system here. No neighbors to hear the crash of broken glass. If the trespassers came in a window...

He grimaced. Two against one wasn't great odds, especially with him armed only with a lamp. He might have time to take out one, but if the other one had a gun...

He finally heard the sirens.

And so did the men on his porch.

They bolted down the wooden steps and seconds later the police cruiser was in his drive. Dennis Marlton pulled in behind them. Lee opened the door and stepped out. "They went that way!"

"Get back inside, Lee!" Ellen called to him. He stepped back and shut the door. Ellen and Carly bounded up the front porch and he let them in.

Marlton and the other officer went in the direction he'd pointed.

"Are you all right?" she asked.

"Yes, I'm fine." He raked a hand through his already mussed hair. "Getting real tired of losing sleep over all this, but I'm fine."

"Join the club on the losing-sleep part."

She paced to the window and peered out, then spun to face him. She winced and held a hand to her head. "Still hurting?"

"Yes. I expect it will for a while. I'm doing my best to ignore it."

"You got my text?"

"I did. I texted you right back. Then called and got no answer so I hopped in my car and headed your way."

"I heard you beep in. I was on the phone with the 911 dispatcher."

"As I was driving over here, I heard the call go out

over the radio." She touched his cheek. "It scared me to death, Lee."

The touch of her soft hand on his skin nearly undid him. How many times had he dreamed of it in prison? Deliberately remembered her smile, her lilting laugh and even her mulish frown when things weren't going her way? He swallowed and held her gaze. She drew in a deep breath and dropped her hand.

"Tell me what happened," she said.

He opened his mouth but was interrupted by a knock on the door. Ellen peeked out then opened it. Dennis Marlton and Louise Donaldson stepped inside. "Did you catch them?" Lee asked.

"No." Louise planted her hands on her hips and drew in one quick breath after the other. She panted and Ellen waited until the woman finally got her breath back. "Now I understand why the chief wanted me on patrol tonight—and why I'm retiring soon."

"What happened to you, Dennis? I thought you were watching the house?"

"I was!"

"And why didn't you answer the phone when I called earlier?" Lee asked.

"What are you talking about? You never called."

"Yes. I did."

Dennis frowned and pulled the device off the clip on his belt and looked at it. He sighed and rubbed his forehead. "I didn't answer the phone because I didn't hear it ring. It's on silent," he said softly. "Sorry."

"And you didn't see the intruders come onto the property?" Ellen asked.

His already flushed cheeks deepened to dark ruddy

red. "I...ah...well...they must have come in from across the yard because I didn't see 'em drive in the driveway."

"But you were supposed to do foot patrols, right?" Louise said.

"Now, look," Dennis blustered, "I was doing my job and I didn't see anything. They came across the backyard. When we chased them, they hopped in a vehicle and took off.

Lee wondered how much chasing actually occurred. What chance did two officers in their sixties have of catching up to the two would-be intruders? Or anyone for that matter? Lee bit his tongue on the words he was tempted to hurl at the man. Instead, he took a calming breath. "Did you get a description?" he asked.

"No," Louise said. "We didn't actually see the car. We just heard it. It was parked on the other side of a house a street over. We made it in time to see the taillights disappear. I called it in and told officers to be watching for it."

"Who else is on duty tonight?" Ellen asked.

"Well. No one, I guess. Eddie Harmon is on the training center that was broken into."

"Right."

Ellen gestured to the living area. "Well, now that we're all here, why don't you tell us what happened, Lee?"

Lee waited until everyone was seated. He stood in front of the mantel and shoved his hands into the front pockets of his sweats. "I had the window open," he said. "I couldn't sleep and voices outside caught my attention. I only heard a few words, it was hard to catch everything, but apparently whoever was out there was looking for something."

"What?" Louise asked.

"I don't know. Not for sure." He looked at Ellen. "But the more I think about it, I think they were looking for the golden retriever puppies."

Ellen straightened. "What? Why?"

"I don't know. But there's a connection. I recognized one of the voices. At first I couldn't place it, but I just realized it was Freddie."

"The vet tech from the Prison Pups program," Ellen said, "the one who shot at us the other day."

"Yes. I told you I got him kicked out of the program for not treating the animals well."

"I remember."

Lee shook his head. "He was mean, but a coward. He would only take a chance like that if there was something big in it for him—like a lot of money."

"Okay."

"I've been thinking about all the people who had access to the German shepherd puppy someone seems to want so bad and also to the three goldens we have. Freddie's the common denominator."

She nodded. "What have you come up with?"

"So you have the veterinarians and the vet techs who initially worked with the dogs. Veronica chipped the German shepherd puppies, right?"

"Right."

"Veronica was killed approximately four months ago," Lee said and held up four fingers as though they needed a visual, "and Sophie took over the facility. The golden retriever puppies had come in just the day before so Sophie inherited them when she took over the program. She then had the pups in the Prison Pups program for some training before she passed the puppies on to Ellen, right?"

Louise shrugged. "That sounds right."

"I'm guessing that Veronica didn't have time to microchip the goldens so maybe the veterinarian working with Sophie did. Who took over Freddie's spot as a vet tech after he was kicked out of the prison program?"

Ellen got on her phone and made a call to find out. "His name is Gerald Nees," she said when she hung up. Her eyes were wide and glittering. "He's also close to getting out of prison."

Lee pursed his lips and let his brain whirl. "The golden retriever puppies were microchipped at the prison. The two vet techs that worked with the dogs were both inmates at the same prison and likely know each other."

"Yes," she said slowly. She lifted a brow. "You think someone put something on the chip while they had access to the puppies."

"Yes. And in order to get the information off that chip, they need to have the dogs."

"I think you may be on to something." Ellen stared at him, admiration gleaming in her eyes. It hit him how badly he wanted her respect. And there it was. It nearly took his breath away.

Ellen's phone rang and the moment was broken. Lee waited for her to check the number. She looked up. "It's the chief. Excuse me a minute." She nodded for Lee to follow, and they walked into his kitchen. "Hello?"

Lee followed and listened to her side of the conversation. "Yes," she said. "That's right." Pause. "Uh-huh. Yes, sir." Another pause. "All right, we'll do that. See you in the morning."

She hung up and turned to Lee. He raised a brow. "Well?"

"The chief wants us to call it a night and come in first thing in the morning to discuss everything."

"Fine."

They walked back into his den and Ellen looked at Dennis Marlton. "Do you mind staying here to finish the shift and then following Lee into the station in the morning?"

"No, I don't mind." He crossed his arms across his belly and his chin jutted. Lee knew the man's pride had been trampled tonight.

"Thanks, Dennis, I appreciate it," Ellen said.

He shrugged and dropped his defensive stance at her soft tones. "Yeah."

Dennis left and Louise followed him, leaving Ellen and Lee alone. She took his hand. "You have to be careful tonight."

"Not much tonight left."

"I was worried when I heard the call come over the radio."

"So you said." He pulled her closer. When she didn't resist, he kept tugging until her lips were a mere centimeter from his. "I'll be careful."

"Good," she whispered.

He covered her lips with his. When she let him deepen the kiss, he slid one hand up her back and under the sloppy ponytail she seemed to love so much. When he lifted his head a fraction she made a sound in her throat. A protest that did wonders for his heart.

He opened his eyes and stared down at her. "We have a lot to talk about when all of this is over."

He heard the husky roughness in his voice and didn't care. His feelings for her had never died. Instead, they'd smoldered, just waiting for her to come back into his life so they could spark into flames once again.

She blinked and stepped back. "Lee—"

He held up a hand. "No, don't say it. I know. I'm sorry. You're my boss."

"Yes, ah…yes. I am."

"I respect that, I promise."

"Good." She nodded. Then seemed to gather her thoughts. "Good. Because we can't let that happen again. This is just a temporary stop for me, Lee. I'm not staying in Desert Valley. Hopefully I'm here long enough to solve your sister's murder and the others and see my mother wake up. Then I'm gone." Her eyes shuttered and he could no longer see her feelings.

Sadness gripped him. She was right and he knew it. Didn't like it, but knew it. "Fine."

"Fine," she echoed.

He grasped her fingers. "I lied."

She blinked up at him. "About what?"

"I'm not sorry about that kiss."

She flushed, pulled her hand from his and walked to the door with Carly at her heels. She gripped the knob and turned back to face him. "I texted Shane. He's going to sit out here the rest of the night."

Shane Weston. Another rookie who'd graduated with Ellen. Lee frowned. "What about Marlton?"

"What about him?"

"I thought he was going to be outside watching."

"He is."

"So?"

"So that's why I asked Shane to be…um…backup." She turned the knob. "See you at the station, Lee."

"See you." He shut the door behind her and leaned his forehead against the wood. What was he *thinking*? What was he *doing*?

Ellen had done it again. She had his brain scrambled.

Was he really going to let himself be hurt again? He let the memories flood over him. Of the hurt Ellen had caused him when she'd chosen her mother over him. Of when she'd left Desert Valley to go to the academy. And now she was back and her presence was threatening to break his heart once again. He sighed and revised his earlier vow. He'd back off. Protect his heart. Because if he didn't, the hurt would be the end of him this time around.

EIGHT

Ellen looked up from her seat in Chief Jones's office and her heart stuttered to see Lee in the doorway. Truly, it had to quit doing that. Carly nudged her hand and she scratched the dog's ears. She always seemed to know when there was a change in Ellen's emotions, and Lee could certainly send them into a tailspin.

In fact, Lee was the one person who could tempt her to revise her plans and stay in this town that her mother ruled. Especially after that kiss last night. Oh, yeah, staying was becoming more and more tempting.

Her heart was wavering. *No!* her mind shouted. Lee had walked away from her once. It would only be a matter of time before he did it again. She really needed to focus on that fact. "Hi."

His eyes landed hers, cool and distant. "Hi."

Confusion flickered through her. What was that about? Was he mad because she'd tensed up and he thought she hadn't wanted him to kiss her? No, that didn't sound like Lee.

She didn't have time to wonder further. The chief slipped into the chair behind his desk and steepled his fingers in front of him. "All right, I spoke with Tristan and Shane earlier. They've worked it out so that the house will be empty tonight."

"That's the woman who works third shift at the hospital?" Ellen asked.

"Yes. We're going to be there tonight when they leave. Tonight's her night off and they're all going out for a family dinner, compliments of the department. They keep their puppy in the laundry room in his kennel when they're not home so we'll be watching to see if anyone goes after him." He looked at Ellen. "You'll be there, too."

"Of course."

Lee shifted as if he wanted to say something. To object or insist on coming along, she couldn't tell.

The chief turned, nodded. "All right, then. Tell me everything about last night."

Ellen blinked. "I think you know most of it."

"Humor me." Ellen nodded and started to speak but before she could, a young woman entered the office. Chief Jones raised a brow. "Yes, Missy?"

Missy had her blond hair pulled up in a loose bun that allowed a few strands to curl around her cheeks. Her green eyes sparkled behind fashionable glasses. "Um. Oh, I need you to sign this form. Carrie said to give it to you."

"Not that one, Missy, this one." Ellen's gaze bounced back to the door where Carrie stood.

"Oh," Missy said. "I'm sorry." She crossed the room and traded papers with Carrie, then walked back to hand it to the chief.

"And," Carrie said, "I told you it could wait until he was finished with his meeting."

"I know." She blinked. "I thought you meant the meeting he just got out of."

"No, Missy, I meant this one." Carrie sighed, a long-suffering sound that had Ellen feeling sorry for Missy and biting her lip against a smile of sympathy for Carrie.

"Right." Missy crossed the room with the signed paper and handed it to Carrie. "I'm sorry."

"Why don't you go answer the phones for a while? I'll handle the rest of the paperwork."

"Of course." Missy slipped away and Carrie shifted then tugged at her dowdy flower-print dress. "I'm sorry, Chief."

"No apologies necessary. She's new. She'll catch on."

"But I hired her."

"And there must have been something about her that told you she could do the job. Give her some time."

Carrie used the tip of her index finger to shove her glasses to the bridge of her nose. "Yes, on paper, she looked great. All right, Chief, thanks." She took a deep breath as though bracing herself then turned and walked out.

"Missy?" Ellen asked, her question directed at Chief Jones.

He nodded. "The new temp. With all of the added workload five new people coming into the department creates, not to mention Veronica's murder, reopening the murder of Ryder Hayes's wife and so on, poor Carrie was really struggling to keep up. It wasn't fair to put that much on her, so I told her to hire someone."

"Missy."

He pursed his lips. "Yeah, Missy." He gave a slight smile. "She's one of the improvements around here made possible by your mother's money."

"Oh."

"Like I said, she'll catch on." He waved a hand. "Moving on."

"All right." Ellen shot a glance at Lee. "I think you're the best one to tell him. After all, I was only there for the tail end of it."

Lee nodded. "It's very simple. I heard voices outside my window, called the cops, they arrived and the two people planning to break in to beat information out of me ran."

"What information were they looking for?"

Lee rubbed his chin. "I have no idea what the information is, but Ellen and I came up with a theory last night that we think is probable."

"What's that?"

Ellen explained.

The chief blew out a breath and leaned back. "Good thoughts, check it out. Take the dogs in and see what's on the chips."

"Great. Thanks." She shot a text to Sophie, asking if she could check the chips later this afternoon, then set aside her phone to focus on her boss.

Chief Jones rubbed his ever-expanding belly. "Look, I know I'm on the fast track to retirement. The whole town knows it." His jaw tightened and his eyes narrowed. "But I want to solve these murders, deaths, whatever, before I go. I need you and the rest of the team to step it up, Ellen. Whatever you need is at your disposal."

Ellen nodded. "I'm glad you said that, Chief."

He lifted a brow. "What do you need?"

"I want to see Veronica's evidence box." She heard Lee pull in a sharp breath.

The chief studied her for a moment. "Okay, sure. You want to tell me why?"

She shrugged. "I don't know. Has anyone looked at it since she died?"

"Of course. Quite a few times."

"Well, I haven't. If you want me to step this up, then humor me."

"All right." He nodded and hefted his bulk from the chair. "Follow me." Lee looked at Ellen and hesitated.

Come on, she mouthed.

Chief Jones led the way to the back of the station and came to a stop before a gray metal door. The supervising clerk wasn't at the desk.

"Where's Alice?" Ellen asked. Alice, a sandy-haired lady in her midfifties, usually sat opposite the door.

"She called in sick today, but it's nothing I can't take care of myself."

"Seems like she's been sick a lot lately."

"Seems like." He signed the log that lay open on the desk, then pulled a set of keys from his front pocket. He unlocked the door and waved them in. "Have a seat at the table."

She did so. Lee sat opposite her and the chief still didn't say anything about Lee being in the room. Was he going to let Lee sit in, as well? Should she insist that he wait outside? Carly shifted at her feet and she let the dog find a comfortable spot. She looked back up, and before she could decide whether or not to bring up the breach of protocol, the chief returned with the evidence box. *Earnshaw, Veronica*, had been written on the end with a black marker. Her case number was in the right-hand corner. The chief set the box on the table in front of her.

Lee bowed his head, and she heard him draw in a

deep breath. She looked at him. Saw the grief in his eyes and wanted to offer words of comfort. But she knew that nothing she could say would lessen the pain of his loss. His hands rested on the table. She leaned over, grasped his fingers and gave them a squeeze, silently asking if he wanted to wait outside.

He met her gaze with reddened eyes. No tears, but she thought he might be on the verge. Then his expression hardened. "Let's take a look."

Ellen nodded, reached over and lifted the lid.

She gasped.

"What is it?" the chief asked.

"It's empty!"

Lee bolted upright in his seat. He'd held back, not sure he could handle seeing what had been left behind at his sister's murder. Ellen's touch had strengthened him, reminded him of his purpose in being there. Now he gazed down into the box, staring at the empty space. "How is this possible?" His head pounded. He glared at the chief, who had paled to an alarming shade of white.

Ellen must have noticed. She jumped to her feet, grabbed his arm and shoved him into her chair. "Chief?"

He swiped an arm across his forehead. "Give me a minute."

"Chief, are you okay? Does your left arm or chest hurt?"

"No, no." He waved a hand. "I'm just in shock. Feel like someone punched me in the gut." He blew out a breath and took another look in the box as though he had to see it again to believe it.

"What happened?" Lee demanded. "Who has access to this area?"

"I do," the chief said. "And so do half a dozen other people. Cops, Alice, Carrie, Missy now. We all have access."

"Unbelievable," Lee muttered, sinking back into his chair.

Ellen's gaze bounced between his and the chief's. "When was the last time someone looked at the evidence?"

Chief Jones sighed. "I looked at it day before yesterday. Let me take a look at the log." He stepped out of the room, grabbed the log then walked back to her and Lee. "Like I thought, I was the last person to look at it. My name is on there two days ago and then again just now."

Ellen glanced at Lee then back at the chief. "I have to ask, Chief. I'm sorry. Did you kill her?" she said, her voice soft, tentative.

Chief Jones blanched. "Ellen? You really have to ask that?"

"You loved her like a daughter. We all know you did." She bit her lip and glanced at Lee before looking back at her boss. "But we all know how Veronica was, too. She could incite a person to do things he'd never believe himself capable of doing. And she was in rare form right before she died."

The chief closed his eyes and breathed a heavy sigh. Lee's muscles tightened even further. Was the man going to confess? Was he sitting across from his sister's killer?

"No," the chief said, opening his eyes. "I didn't kill her. I don't know what was going on with her before she died. I don't know why she was like she was period. Probably had something to do with the way you grew up." He shot an apologetic look at Lee. "No offense, but your parents' history isn't exactly confidential."

"No offense taken," Lee murmured. "You were there for her, a male role model who was able to reel her in sometimes when she was going too far overboard with her snarkiness and wild ways. She loved you, even said if she could have handpicked a father, she would have chosen you."

The chief swallowed and his eyes reddened. "But unfortunately, she didn't confide in me about a lot of things, so I don't know who she antagonized enough to kill her." He met Lee's gaze. "But it wasn't me."

Lee looked at Ellen and she nodded. He could see her mind spinning. "So," she said, "only police and employees of the station have access." She cleared her throat. "You know, your new hire isn't the brightest bulb on the strand. Is it possible someone could have slipped past her and gained access to the evidence room? Maybe when you and Carrie were out?"

"But the person would need a key to get in."

"Where are the keys kept?"

"I have a set on me at all times and...in a drawer." He held up a hand. "And before you ask, no, the drawer isn't always locked."

Lee held on to his temper. How had this place not been shut down? Or at least cleaned out by now?

Ellen paced in front of the table, "I'm not going to address that one. Let's talk about what we know. It's common knowledge that Veronica was microchipping the puppies the night she died. She told James that she'd be over to his house to help with a training issue when she was finished."

The chief nodded. "Right."

"The two German shepherd puppies found the night of her murder had already been scanned and they show the station address. Nothing odd there. It's what we expected to find. However, since we've come up with our theory that the goal of the attempted break-in at Lee's was to get the three golden puppies that were microchipped at the prison, I don't think it's a stretch to believe that Veronica was interrupted by the killer and might have managed to chip the third German shepherd puppy with some information about her killer."

"Which would be why she fought so hard to make sure the puppy got out of the fence," Lee said. "I think she was trying to send a message—that she put some information on Marco's chip."

Ellen nodded. "So Veronica dragged herself from the clinic to the gate and let the third puppy, Marco, escape just in case the killer figured out what she was doing and got rid of the puppies."

"I think Veronica was hoping the puppy she'd chipped with the killer's information would be found and her killer brought to justice," Lee said. Chief Jones's head swiveled back and forth between them. "And I think it's reasonable to deduce that the killer might have come to this conclusion, as well."

"Which would explain all the break-ins around town," Ellen said. "The killer is looking for the puppy to get rid of it and any evidence Veronica might have planted on it."

"So where's the puppy?" Lee asked. "It's got that distinct marking on its head, it should be easy enough to spot. How do you hide an eight-month-old puppy? And why would you do it anyway?"

"For several possible reasons. One," Ellen said, "whoever took the puppy has come to love it. And if the person knows that the police are looking for it—and with the

flyers all over town, how could this person *not* know—
he or she may not want to give it up now."

"Or, two," Lee said, "the person has sold it to someone
who lives out of town and we'll never find it."

"Or that. But I don't know. There was a witness who
saw a person on a bicycle pick the puppy up and ride
off with it. A bicycle would indicate someone in town
has that puppy."

"And, not to be the voice of doom, but it could have
run off and gotten hit by a car or just not have survived."

Ellen grimaced. "I was trying not to think of that
one."

Lee rubbed a hand across his eyes. He was so ready
for this craziness to be over. "Let's keep going on the assumption that the puppy is still alive and out there somewhere. I think we need to get a plea out for this person
to return the puppy, that it's needed in an ongoing investigation and could be the only key to solving a murder."

The chief nodded. "We can do that."

Ellen placed the top back on the empty box. "I'll put
this back. Let's not let on that we know the evidence is
missing."

"All right." The chief was eager to agree to that one,
Lee noticed sourly. "What are you thinking?"

"Just that I want to keep this under our hats for now."

"Fine." Chief Jones swiped his forehead again with
his sleeve.

"Are you sure you're all right, sir?" Ellen asked him.

"Just reeling right now. I've been in this business a
long time and this case just beats all I've ever seen."

"I know, but we'll figure it out. It might not happen as
fast as we'd like, but we will." Ellen picked up the box.
"I'll be right back."

She walked down the aisle and Lee could see her looking for the right spot.

"I'm sorry about your sister, son."

Lee looked into the chief's eyes. "I know."

"You've had it pretty rough in this town."

"Yes." He really didn't feel like small talk.

"I also want to apologize for Ken's involvement in sending you to prison. If I'd known anything about that, I would have intervened."

Lee sighed. "I believe you." And he found he did. Out of the corner of his eye, he saw Ellen stoop down and reach for something. "What is it?" he called.

She slid a hand in between two of the metal shelves. "This."

NINE

Ellen pulled her hand back and stared at the shiny object that had caught her eye.

Lee and the chief walked up beside her. "What is it?" Lee asked.

"An earring." Ellen studied the pretty pearl with the simple gold clip.

"What's that doing there?"

"I don't know. That's a really good question. There's no dust on it so I wouldn't think it's been here long." She looked up. "Chief, look at these cases here and tell me which ones are open and currently being investigated."

He stepped forward and studied the names on the boxes. "Huh. On this rack, it holds cases with last names starting with *A* to *E* so that would just be Veronica's."

"What about this rack?"

"This is *F* to *J*, so Melanie Hayes is the only case anyone would be actively investigating."

"And her box is on the other end of the shelves."

"What are you thinking?"

"Just trying to put this together, figure out where the person would be standing for the earring to drop off and land here." Ellen raked a hand down her ponytail. "Well, it's a given that whoever came in with the intention of stealing the evidence didn't sign the log. But at least we have a time line. The stuff was stolen either yesterday or early this morning. Can we check the security cameras?"

Chief Jones nodded. "Yes, I'll pull up the footage and we can start going through it."

She looked at the earring again. "I know I touched this, Chief, but do you think the lab could try to get some DNA off the part that hooks to the ear?"

"I think it's a long shot, but bag it and note that you handled it." He walked to a drawer and pulled out an evidence bag. She dropped the earring into it and snagged a marker from the cup on the shelf. She noted she'd handled the earring, wishing she'd grabbed a glove or something to pick it up, but she hadn't even thought that what she was seeing was evidence. Kicking herself wasn't going to help anything. She handed the bag to the chief.

"I'll have Carrie get this on its way." He paused. "Actually, I'll ask Missy to do it. It's something easy and I think she needs to do something right in Carrie's eyes."

"You think that's wise? It's possible someone inside this office stole the evidence."

He hesitated. "I'll call ahead and let them know she's bringing it—and I'll let Missy know that I've called ahead. Hold on a second." He disappeared into the lobby area. When he came back he nodded to the door at the end of the hall. "Let's go look at the footage."

Lee had been awfully quiet during everything, just watching and listening. She glanced at him with a raised brow. He just shook his head. They followed the chief into another small area that housed the security computers. He sat in front of the nearest one and clicked the mouse. "Newfangled stuff. Let's hope it's worth all the money the good citizens of Desert Valley put into it."

Surprisingly, he managed to bring the footage up without much trouble or backtracking. He muttered a lot, but Ellen could deal with that if she got to see the video.

"There." On the screen, a figure dressed in black approached the evidence room door, inserted the key and was inside faster than Ellen could blink.

"Well," she said. "There you go."

"Black hoodie, black pants, black gloves. Never looks up at the camera, never hesitates," Lee said.

"And now the door is opening," the chief said, "and the person is coming out. Again, never looks at the camera and the hoodie disguises any features. I can't even tell if it's a man or a woman." He slapped the desk in disgust.

Carly jumped and stood. Ellen placed a hand on the dog's ears and gave her a scratch of reassurance. Satisfied, Carly laid back on the floor and settled her head between her paws once more.

"What about the camera inside the room?" Ellen asked. "Could we see if maybe the person pushed the hoodie back or something while he or she was in there?" Chief Jones didn't answer. "Sir?"

His cheeks flushed and Ellen knew she wasn't going to like what he had to say. "It stopped working about a week ago and hasn't been repaired yet." Ellen stared at him. He sighed and rubbed his eyes. "I know. You don't need to say anything."

She bit her lip. So many cases could have been compromised. But that wasn't her problem. She had to focus on finding Veronica's killer. "All right. I won't say anything."

"It'll be fixed by tomorrow."

Unfortunately, that was too late for them. "Okay," she sighed. "At least this hasn't been a complete waste of time." She bit her lip and looked at the chief. "Chief, I know you think it's a long shot to find anything on the earring, but I say there's always hope." She paused and frowned. "What would make the person steal the evidence now? Why not months ago when the evidence was placed in the room?"

The chief shook his head. "I don't know. There wasn't any new evidence in there, but we've been pulling that box pretty regularly, going over and over the material in there. Maybe it was making someone nervous."

"Or it was the camera," Ellen said. "The person knew the camera was broken inside the evidence room. Getting in and out without being detected would be a breeze with that camera not working." She paused and tapped her chin, then leaned forward. "What if it was just simply a moment of opportunity for this person? He, or she—" she said with a nod to the chief, "—saw his, or her—" she held up the earring "—chance and grabbed it."

"Could be," the chief said.

Ellen nodded. "What if we start focusing on our suspect in a different light?"

"What kind of light?"

"What if we start thinking the killer is a woman?"

"A woman who was angry at Veronica?"

"Or even jealous?" Ellen asked. "She seemed to have a history with just about every man in town." She cut her eyes to Lee. "Sorry."

He shrugged, but she saw the pain there. "It's true."

"Jealous of Veronica?" Chief Jones let out a low, humorless chuckle. "Honey, that's three-fourths of the Desert Valley female population."

Ellen resisted rolling her eyes and rubbed them instead. "I know, but maybe coming at this case from a different perspective will allow us to see things a little differently. Maybe it will shake something loose. The fact that the person obviously had a key sounds a huge alarm for me. It's possible this is an inside job."

"Or someone was able to steal a key from one of the DVPD personnel." Chief Jones shrugged. "All right. I'll notify the other rookies and tell them we might be looking for a woman. Sure can't hurt. It's not like we're overrun with male suspects. At least not ones we haven't already cleared."

"Great." Her phone buzzed. She glanced at the screen. "That's a text from Sophie."

"What'd she say?"

Ellen read the message. "She said she's not at the facility today, but she can check the puppies' chips first thing in the morning." She gave a nod. "That'll work. We'll do the stakeout tonight and then take the puppies in to Sophie in the morning."

She stood. Chief Jones did, as well. "You're a good cop, Ellen."

She raised a brow. "Thanks, Chief."

He cleared his throat. "I've…ah…let things go. Too many things. I'll make sure that camera's fixed ASAP."

She nodded. "Good." Carly joined her, and they headed for the exit.

As she and Lee passed through into the lobby, Ellen noticed Carrie at the reception desk. "Thanks for your help, Carrie."

The woman looked up. "You're welcome. Again, I apologize for Missy." She glanced at the glass door where Missy was just walking down the steps. Probably on her way to mail off the earring. "Honestly, she looked great on paper. I'm not sure what happened."

"It's not your fault, Carrie. Sometimes you just have to work with someone awhile before you can know their strengths and weaknesses."

"Well..." She pursed her lips. "Not to be ugly, but I don't think I'm going to have any trouble ascertaining her weaknesses." She sighed. "So I'll just have to look for her strengths and work with those, right?" She flashed a smile and adjusted her glasses.

"That's the spirit."

Carrie laughed. "Right." She cut her eyes to Lee. "Good to see you, Lee."

He nodded at her. "You too, Carrie."

"So sorry about Veronica. It's just unbelievable that someone in this town could do such a thing."

He gave her a tight smile. "I know. Thanks for the condolences."

Ellen felt Lee's hand on her back and figured he was ready to get out of the station. When they stepped outside, the dry heat hit her. As did the feeling of being watched. She sucked in a breath and glanced at her phone. "I've got an appointment with a client in ten minutes." She looked up and let her gaze roam. Was someone watching her and Lee right now?

"I'll walk over to the center with you."

As they walked, Ellen examined everyone she passed. Their faces and their body language. No one stood out as particularly interested in her. Other than the usual attention she and Carly attracted.

"Will it be dangerous?" Lee asked.

Ellen glanced at him. "What?"

"The stakeout."

"Probably not. Stakeouts are usually pretty boring in spite of what you see on television."

"But if they show up?"

"We nab him. We'll far out number them."

"True. There will more of you than them."

She stopped at the door of the training center. "Are you worried?"

"Why would I be worried? This is what you're trained to do, remember?"

She heard the underlying thread of sarcasm and grimaced. "Yes, I am." They went inside and Ellen saw her client sitting in the waiting area. "We'll talk later."

"I'm going to check on my truck and work with Dash for a bit, but we'll definitely talk later."

She watched him walk away.

Now, what did that mean?

Lee held Dash in the crook of his arm and stopped on his way to the training yard to watch Ellen work with the client and the dog. She was amazing. And incredibly patient. Which was funny to him because he knew she had not been blessed with an abundance of that particular trait. But somehow she found an extra measure of it whenever she worked with the dogs and her clients.

Lee found a handful of treats and tucked them into his front pocket. He made his way to the nearest outdoor training yard. There were three indoor training areas, but he preferred to be outside. He chose the puppy-run area as there were fewer distractions there than the other with the obstacle course–like objects.

He set the puppy down, grabbed a tennis ball from the bucket near the door and threw it. Dash let out a happy bark and took off after it. He'd let the dog run off some energy before getting down to business.

It was hot, but it felt good to be outside in the sun. He'd spent too much time in a prison cell. Being outside no matter what kind of weather was always a healing balm to his wounded spirit.

With the woods to his left and around the back of the center, he also relished the privacy. Being around other inmates day in and day out with no time to just be alone had been one of the hardest things for him to adjust to. And truthfully, he never had. He'd just endured and drawn as little attention to himself as possible. That course of action had worked relatively well and he had to admit, he'd probably come out of prison as unscathed as was possible.

He took several treats from his pocket even as he tossed the ball again. It rolled against the fence at the far side of the run.

Dash bolted after it and clamped down on it. He started to bring it back to Lee, then spun back toward the fence, the ball dropping from his mouth. He raced to the fence and barked. Then rose up on his hind legs and continued his high-pitched yapping.

"Dash. Come!"

The dog ignored him, his full attention on the woods just beyond the fence.

Uneasiness slithered through Lee. "Dash! Come!" Was someone in the woods watching? He narrowed his eyes and let his gaze run the length of the woods. He saw nothing that alarmed him but decided to use common sense and be safe. "Come!"

Dash dropped to all fours and turned to look at him,

then whirled back to the fence to voice his displeasure at whatever was out there.

"Lee?"

Lee turned to see Ellen come out the access door and into the yard. "Hey."

"What's going on?"

"He's going nuts. I think someone may be in the woods out there past the fence."

Her hand went to her weapon. "With all that's been going on, we don't want to take any chances. Let's get him back inside. I'll get Carly and we'll go investigate."

He frowned. "Be careful."

"Always."

She waited, standing guard while he gathered the wriggling puppy and carried him inside.

Once back in the protection of the facility, Ellen took off for the exit that would lead her toward the woods.

TEN

Ellen walked toward the woods, her weapon a comforting weight in her hand. She didn't like being so exposed as she crossed the expanse of yard to the tree line. Carly trotted beside her, her ears raised, nose quivering.

Ellen spoke into the radio on her shoulder. "Suspicious activity in the east woods of the Canyon County K-9 Training Center. Request backup."

Her radio crackled softly. "Ellen, this is Tristan. I'm on the way out there."

"What's your ETA?"

"I'm just up the street. Give me two minutes."

He was close. "Meet me at the edge of the woods." She looked down, studying the ground. It was dry and hot, but she thought she found a shoe imprint. Maybe. "Carly, track." She knelt and pointed. Carly sniffed. Her sides quivered.

"Don't do anything until I get there," Tristan said.

"I'm not, but Carly's going tracking."

She held the end of the leash in her left hand, her weapon in her right. Carly's ears swiveled and something just ahead in the woods caught her attention. She let Carly take the lead. The dog pulled her closer and

Ellen felt much better when she slipped into the protection of the tree line.

At least the trees covered her somewhat. But she knew that even though she wore a vest, it wouldn't offer any protection against a head shot.

Her radio crackled to life again and she plugged her earpiece in. "I'm here," Tristan said. "Coming through the woods from the side."

"I'm just inside the tree line near the fence. Work your way around toward me. I'm going to let Carly loose and see what she can find."

"Stay covered. Don't let him get a shot at you."

If there was a him. She was going on the assumption there was someone with a gun in the woods somewhere. "That's the idea." She fell silent and her gaze scanned the trees, between them, around them and beyond. She was looking for any kind of movement, something to indicate someone was hiding.

And got nothing. She unhooked Carly's leash. She didn't know if Carly had gotten anything from the shoe print, but maybe she'd find something anyway. "Seek."

Carly lifted her nose into the air, then took off through the woods. Ellen followed, watching the dog as she sniffed the ground. Every so often she'd raise her head. Finally she stopped and sat. Ellen walked over and squatted next to the dog. "You find something, girl?"

Carly jumped at the tree next to her then sat again.

Ellen looked up. A dark T-shirt had been tossed over a branch about a foot above her. "Good job, Carly." She slipped the dog a treat.

Ellen rose and turned in a circle. Stopped and listened. Watched. So there had been someone in the trees. He'd tossed the shirt in order to throw Carly off the scent. Or at least slow her down a bit.

A snapping sound to her right. Her head swiveled. Her fingers tightened around the grip of her weapon. "Police! Show yourself!"

"It's just me, Ellen," Tristan called.

The breath whooshed from her and she lowered her weapon. Tristan stepped out from behind the tree followed by Jesse. "He's gone," Ellen said.

"Did you see him?"

"Nope." She sighed and tucked her gun into her holster. "He was probably gone before you even got here."

"Maybe. He had to have had a vehicle waiting."

"That seems to be his MO. He always has some kind of escape plan ready and waiting."

Tristan held up a gloved hand. He held something that looked like a piece of material.

"What's that?" she asked.

"Not sure. Part of his shirt or something."

"Could it have been there awhile?"

He sniffed it. "Has a hint of fabric softener on it so I'm going to say it's recent."

"Think it could match that?" She pointed up.

His gaze followed and he nodded. "It's the same color."

"Let's send it off to Flagstaff and have the lab analyze it. Maybe they'll find something."

"You don't sound too hopeful."

"And you are?"

He gave a low laugh, grabbed the shirt from the branch with his gloved hand and held it up. "There. It's ripped." He held up the small piece. "I'd say that's a perfect match."

Ellen sighed. "He knew we'd have the dogs if he got caught."

"Yeah. And knew exactly how to slow them down."

Together they walked back to the edge of the woods. When they stepped into the clearing, she looked toward the building and could see Lee coming toward her.

He met them halfway. "Nothing?"

"No. Someone was definitely out there, but we don't have a clue who it was."

"Well," Tristan said, "we have a little clue, but we're not sure it'll tell us much." He showed Lee the bit of fabric.

Lee sighed. "Great." Then his jaw tightened and he nodded to the building. "I'll use one of the indoor training yards. I've got work to do."

Tristan clapped Ellen on the shoulder. "See you tonight."

"Just after dark."

She prayed that the stakeout worked and they caught the person after the puppies. Because if they didn't, she wasn't sure what the next step would be. But the feeling in her gut said if they didn't catch this person soon, someone else was going to get hurt. Or killed.

Lee stepped back inside the assistance center and made his way to the indoor training yard. He could tell by the way Ellen and Tristan walked and talked, there was no longer any threat outside. He carried the puppy to the center of the area and pulled a treat from his pocket. "Sit."

Dash sat.

"Stay."

Lee held the treat in front of him and walked backward. The puppy squirmed, but stayed put.

"Come."

Dash bolted to sit in front of him and Lee gave him the treat, then pulled a rope toy from his pocket for a game of tug-of-war. He tossed the puppy the end and Dash clamped down on it with glee in his brown eyes. Lee pulled hard enough to challenge the little guy, but not so hard he pulled him off balance.

He heard footsteps behind him and turned to find Ellen watching. She gave him a small smile. "You're looking good."

He blinked. "Sorry?"

Her cheeks pinked. "You and Dash. You're looking good. Together. As in he's responding well to your training."

"Oh. Thanks." He relished the praise then forced himself to shove aside the feeling. She was his boss. And she was leaving town after this assignment was over. He cleared his throat. "Hope the stakeout goes well."

"Me, too." She looked away then back. "I don't like this tension between us, Lee."

"I don't, either."

"So what do we do about it?"

He shrugged. "I don't know, Ellen. I've got to keep myself at a distance. You're leaving and I don't need another broken heart."

His honesty seemed to leave her at a loss for words. Frankly, he was surprised he'd let the words pass through his lips. She simply stared at him, her throat working. "Right."

Once again Lee wished he'd kept his mouth shut. Then again, part of him was glad it was out there. He stepped forward and touched her cheek. "Ellen, you're amazing. The determination you've shown to branch out on your own and out from under your mother, the career path you've chosen, this." He waved a hand to indicate the assistance center. "You've got an incredible future ahead of you. I'm not going to do anything to come between you and that."

She nodded, and looked away from him. "And you still need to finish vet school."

"One day."

She met his eyes again. "One day soon, Lee."

"Yes, that's the plan."

She nodded and Carly nudged her thigh. She reached down and scratched the dog's ears while Lee processed the fact that Ellen might once again be walking out of his life and soon.

His intention had been to let her do so in order to spare himself a broken heart.

Unfortunately, he'd just discovered he was too late to avoid that.

Ellen leaned her head back against the headrest and glanced over at Tristan. "How's the kid sister?"

He blew out a sigh, then took a sip of coffee from the thermos he'd brought. Ellen had one, too, but she hadn't needed the caffeine. Thoughts of Lee were enough to keep her adrenaline racing. Tristan lifted a shoulder in a light shrug. "Mia. She's…hanging out with the wrong crowd, secretive, argumentative. She's…struggling."

"And you are, too?"

"Yeah."

"I'm sorry."

Another shrug. "I keep hoping she'll come around and see that I'm not the bad guy in her life."

"She will. Just be patient."

"That's the plan."

She spoke into her radio to Shane and James, who were parked just a bit farther down the street with a different view of the house. They could see the backyard while she and Tristan covered the front. "Nothing here. How about you guys?"

"All's quiet."

"Think this is a waste of time?"

"Probably," Shane grumbled in her ear.

She sighed and shot a look back over at Tristan. He was a good-looking guy with his brown hair and blue eyes. If she had to be attracted to someone, why couldn't it be someone like him? Someone who understood her job? Someone she didn't have any baggage with?

"What is it? You're staring."

She blinked. "Oh. Sorry, just thinking."

"About?"

"A lot of things. Men. Life."

He gave a low chuckle but she noticed he kept his eyes on the house. "It's not any greener on the other side, Ellen. No matter what man you wind up with, he's going to have his issues."

She gaped. "Did I speak my thoughts out loud?"

"You didn't have to. I've watched you and Lee over the past couple of days. I know you guys have a history together." At her frown, he shrugged. "Word travels fast in a small town. I can see you struggling and wish I could help."

"But you can't."

"Nope. I'm not one to get involved in other people's love lives. This is between you and Lee."

"And my mother," she muttered.

He frowned. "What?"

"Nothing. Just…nothing. And I don't have a love life."

He gave a low chuckle. "Yes, you do."

"Do not."

"Okay, if you say so."

"I say so."

He fell silent, but she heard him whisper under his breath, "But you do."

The next three hours passed mostly in silence. Just like she told Lee it would be, the stakeout was quiet and boring.

Finally, they told the family to come home and they waited until they were safely inside.

Tristan pulled away from the curb. "Thanks," Ellen said.

"For what?"

She gave him a soft smile. "Just thanks."

Ellen knew she needed to figure out what to do about Lee, but Tristan was right. Everyone had issues, battles to fight in life. She just had to decide if she wanted to do that with Lee. In Desert Valley.

The sinking in her stomach at the thought of living near her mother was the answer to that question.

ELEVEN

The next morning Ellen swung by Lee's and picked him up. Things were quiet between them, but not uncomfortable. "Sophie texted me earlier to let me know she's at the center and we can come on in," Ellen told him.

"Great. Nothing happened last night? I haven't heard anything on the news," he said as he climbed into her SUV. "I figured if you caught the person responsible for all the break-ins, I would have heard about it." Carly greeted him with a swipe of her tongue. Lee scratched her ears and she settled back on the seat.

"No. It was a bust."

"Are you all going to try again?"

"Yes. Tristan and Shane are arranging to do it again tonight with the other home owner."

"Good."

She wasn't going to bring up anything personal. Not now. They were on the way to the assistance center, which was only a five-minute drive from Lee's house. When she pulled up in front, Lee opened his door. "I'll get the dogs if you want to wait here."

Ellen shook her head. "I'm going to come in for a few minutes and check on things. I need to make a phone call, too." She'd been thinking about their visit with the chief ever since she'd walked out of the station yesterday.

He nodded and disappeared inside. She pulled her phone from her pocket and dialed Ryder Hayes's number. He answered. "Hayes."

"Ryder, this is Ellen. I need to know if you ever investigated Chief Jones during the time of Veronica's murder."

"No, I don't think we officially investigated him, but we didn't have to. He was at his birthday dinner when he got the call about Veronica's death."

"Ah. Okay, so an airtight alibi?"

"Definitely."

"Good to know, thanks."

"Want to tell me why?"

"It's not important now. If you truly want to know, I'll fill you in later."

"Okay. Anything else?"

"Nope. Talk to you soon."

She hung up and walked inside the assistance center. Just like every time, she felt a jolt of happiness flow through her. Here something good was happening. Here people found a reason to smile again. She walked into the training area and found two of her employees working. One had Frisbee, a recent rescue, on a leash and was teaching him to retrieve items dropped from a wheelchair. The other worker, with a blindfold on, had Samson, a beautiful Lab, guiding her through an obstacle course. Satisfaction filled Ellen. Soon these two dogs would be ready to help others.

"You ready?"

She turned to find Lee with the three puppies leashed and ready to go. Dash strained toward the door, ready for his next adventure. King and Lady sniffed Ellen's shoes. "Sure."

Together, they walked them over to the K-9 Unit Training Center. Once inside, Ellen went to find Sophie while Lee waited in the lobby.

"Sophie? You here?" She went to the office first and found it empty. She walked out into the nearest training yard and found Sophie with a German shepherd puppy on a leash. They would walk, then Sophie would stop and give a command. If the puppy obeyed, he got a treat.

"Hey, Sophie, we're here."

Sophie looked up. "Hey, Ellen, what's going on? You weren't real clear about what's happening other than you want me to read the chips on the dogs."

"Yesterday we were talking with Chief Jones and think we may have a lead on the attempted break-in at Lee's the other night."

"Hey, yeah, I heard about that. Everything okay?"

"For now. We brought the three puppies you donated to my training center. We just wanted to make sure the chips say what they're supposed to say."

"Of course. Give me a few minutes to finish up here and I'll get right on it. You can put the dogs in the kennel if you want to come back later."

"We'll just wait. Thanks."

Ellen returned to find Lee working with the puppies in his own special way. "Down," he said as he pointed to the floor. When Dash dropped his hind end to the floor, Lee smiled and slipped the puppy a treat.

"He makes those disappear fast," Ellen said.

Lee nodded. "He's a smart one."

"Sophie said she'd be right out. She's going to check the chips while we wait."

"Great."

"Lee, I know the others have asked you this, but—"

He looked up. "But?"

"But can you think of anyone else who would have it in for Veronica? Females, I mean?"

He sighed. "I've thought long and hard on that. I mean, she was only nice to people who could do something for her. I don't mean to talk ill of her, but we both know how she was."

"I know."

"Yesterday, I honestly thought Chief Jones was going to confess that he'd killed her in a fit of rage or something."

"I wondered about that myself, but I don't think he did it. He has an airtight alibi anyway."

"How do you know?"

"I checked."

"Right."

"And they've ruled out her ex-husband, William Pennington."

"Yes." Lee frowned and pursed his lips. "I can't believe everything he was into. A drug runner, of all things."

"I know, I think that came as quite a shock to a number of people."

Lee sighed. "And Lloyd Harglow had an airtight alibi." Veronica had been seeing Lloyd while still married to Pennington.

"Any other ex-boyfriends out there?"

He shrugged. "I'm not the one to ask. Veronica didn't come to visit very often while I was in prison."

"I'm sorry."

"I am, too. Now."

"So the women," Ellen said. "What woman might want to kill Veronica?"

"Well, I'm sure Lloyd Harglow's wife wasn't too fond of Veronica for cheating with him. What about her?"

"We checked her. And while she hated Veronica, she didn't kill her."

"Another airtight alibi?"

"Afraid so."

Sophie stepped into the area. "I can check the puppies now if you want to bring them into the room."

Lee stood and walked the puppies behind Sophie into a lab-like area. She picked up a device and held it over Dash's neck. Then King's, then Lady's. She wrote each of the numbers down and handed the paper to Ellen. "All the puppies are showing as belonging to the Canyon County Prison."

Lee closed his eyes and blew out a breath. Ellen felt her shoulders droop. "Well, that was a bust."

Ellen studied the paper. "Maybe not." She held it out so he could see it. "Look at these ID numbers. Two are pretty similar, but one is a bit different. It's Dash's number."

Lee looked. "You're right. It's very different. I wonder why."

Ellen studied Sophie's intense expression as she stared at the little golden puppy. Sophie tapped her lip. "What is it?" Ellen asked.

"Just thinking why that number would be so off."

Lee frowned. "Could it be some kind of code?"

"Maybe." Ellen looked at Sophie.

"I didn't chip these puppies. The vet next door and her tech did. Veronica already had the puppies before she died. I just inherited them. When you told me your plans to start up your facility, I thought they'd make a good addition."

"And they do, thanks." She looked at Lee. "Why don't we see if we can talk to Tanya a bit about this?"

"All right." He rubbed the back of his head.

"What are you thinking?" she asked.

"Tanya Fowler's clinic at the prison is where Freddie and I would help out. I know Dr. Fowler. The thing is, I can't see her doing anything illegal, but if I've calculated the timing right, Freddie would have been out of the program before the puppies were chipped."

"Okay, so it wasn't Freddie who did it." She paused then said, "Could it possibly be the other inmate who's working in the Prison Pups program?"

Lee shrugged. "It's worth finding out."

"But if someone is putting inmates in this particular position with the intention of microchipping dogs with messages or something, that means someone at the prison is involved."

"Or Ken Bucks arranged for it."

"True." She pursed her lips then nodded. "Let's go talk to Tanya."

Lee and Ellen walked the dogs next door to the veterinarian's office. The air-conditioning was a welcome respite from the heat of the day. A man in uniform, identifying himself as a corrections officer, sat in the waiting area reading a magazine. Lee blinked. He knew him from the prison. Another younger man in a lab coat stood behind the desk. When he looked up, his eyes widened slightly before he glanced back down at the computer. "Help you?"

"Is Tanya around?" Lee asked. He noticed the tattoos on the man's fingers.

"Sure, I'll get her." He practically bolted from the room and into the back.

Lee looked at Ellen and she raised a brow. "What was that about?"

"I don't know. Good question."

Tanya appeared in the doorway. "Hey, Ellen, Lee, what can I do for you?"

Ellen nodded to the back. "I see you've gotten a new tech."

"Yes, Gerald Nees. He started working here about a month ago on a work-release program."

"I thought I recognized him," Lee said. "He's an inmate."

"Yes, but he's due to be released in just a few weeks and he met all the requirements for the program." She nodded her head to the man in the chair to their right. "That's Phillip Carr. He's a prison guard. He brings Gerald in for several hours a day for his shift to help with the dogs."

Officer Carr looked up at the mention of his name and gave them a short nod.

"Is Gerald the one who chipped these goldens?" Ellen asked Tanya.

"He could be. Are these the three Sophie donated to your program?"

"Yes."

"Then, he would have been the one." She looked at Lee. "As you know, I had to fire Freddie. That left me quite short staffed so I asked about a replacement. Gerald looked great on paper other than his incarceration issue." She gave them a wry smile.

"'Looking good on paper' seems to be a popular thing these days," Lee muttered.

Ellen shot him an exasperated look and he shrugged.

"Anyway," Tanya said, "Gerald had expressed an interest in working with animals, and since he'd kept his nose clean while in prison, we decided to give him a chance."

Lee pulled the paper with the ID numbers on them from his pocket. "Can you tell me why this number would be so different from the other two?"

Tanya looked at them and frowned. "No, that's weird. If the dogs were chipped at the same time then all three numbers should be sequential. See these two? This one ends in the number one. The next one ends in two and the last one should end in either zero or three. But it doesn't." She shook her head. "You've got all these letters and numbers mixed in. This really doesn't make sense."

A low thud sounded and Tanya's eyes went wide. Lee blinked as she gasped and slowly sank to the floor.

"Tanya!" Ellen rushed to the vet when another thunk echoed. This time the prison guard mimicked Tanya's actions and slid from his seat to the floor. "Lee! Get down!"

For a fraction of a second, he stared at the dart protruding from the guard's chest. And he realized someone was shooting at them. He released the dogs and spun to the door to see Gerald aiming for his next victim—Ellen.

TWELVE

Lee lunged toward the inmate, who backpedaled and turned the weapon on him. Gerald pulled the trigger and Lee hit the floor rolling. Lee heard the dart slam into the wall behind him. With a swipe of his left foot, he caught Gerald in the back of his right knee. The man hollered and went down.

"Police! Freeze! Drop the weapon now!"

Gerald ignored Ellen's orders and once again tried to get a bead on Lee. Then the weapon was flying through the air to land with a clatter on the floor behind Gerald.

Gerald screamed and grabbed his wrist. "You broke it!"

"Get on the floor!" Ellen gave him another shove, and he fell onto his stomach. She landed on his back with her knee and Lee heard the breath whoosh from the man's lungs. Before he could blink she had his hands cuffed behind his back. Gerald still hollered about his wrist. Lee hoped it was painful.

She rose to her feet and kept her weapon trained on the gasping man. "Lee, you okay?"

"Yes. You?"

"Yeah. Call 911."

Lee rolled to his feet in a smooth movement and jumped the counter to grab the phone and punch in the numbers. As close as the police department was, backup would be here quickly.

He gave the information requested and asked for an ambulance. He heard the dispatcher yell something, then come back on the line. "Chief Jones just ran out the door. He's on the way there, too."

"Thanks." He hung up and moved to the unconscious prison guard. Ellen was still bent over the vet. "How's Tanya?"

"Out cold, but her pulse is strong. She's breathing okay."

"What were they shot with?" He checked Phillip's pulse and found it strong, as well.

"Looks like a tranquilizer dart—the one weapon Gerald could get his hands on."

Sirens sounded. Gerald fought the cuffs. "Let me go, you have no right!"

Ellen ignored him. Lee wanted to knock the breath out of him again.

The door burst open and Chief Jones stepped inside. Sweat rolled down his red cheeks, his breath came in pants. "What happened here?"

"Gerald went a little crazy," Ellen said. "Where's the ambulance."

"On the way."

Ellen stood and swiped a hand down her face. "I think they'll be all right. It was a tranquilizer gun. I think they were mild darts, but they definitely need to be checked out."

Chief Jones knelt by Phillip, the prison guard, and laid his fingers on the man's neck. "Still strong."

Ellen did the same once more with Tanya. "Hers, too."

The chief sank into a chair and stared at Gerald. "So. What set him off?"

Lee's gaze bounced between Gerald and the three goldens who'd crawled under the chairs on the far side of the room and were busy chewing on their leashes.

"The dogs," Lee said.

"What?"

"He was shocked to see them come in. At first, I thought it might have been me, but it was the dogs. I'm going to guess he's working for the people who are after them."

Ellen nodded. "And I'll also hazard a guess that he made a phone call soon after we got here."

Chief Jones nodded. "I'll check the phone records." He looked at Gerald. "So what do you have to say for yourself?"

Gerald tightened his lips and glared. The chief stared at him. "I got nothing to say to any of you," Gerald finally snarled.

The ambulance pulled up to the door and Chief Jones stood and hitched his belt. "Fine. We'll hash it out at the station."

"We won't hash out nothing. I'm not talking. Talking gets you dead." His glare intensified. "And after today, I can promise you're all next."

Ellen glanced at Lee. He was barely holding his temper in check and she didn't blame him. Finally they had someone in custody who might know something about Veronica's murder. The chief hauled Gerald to his feet. Paramedics rushed in and Ellen directed them to the two who needed them. While they worked on them, she followed Chief Jones and Gerald outside. Red lights flashed on top of the emergency vehicles. "I want to question him, Chief."

"Get in line." He hauled the man into the back of the cruiser.

"I need to see a doctor," Gerald grumbled. "I think she broke a rib."

Gerald glared up at her. Ellen stared back without a blink. He finally looked away and she glanced up to see the chief watching. A small smile played around the corners of his lips and she lifted a brow. He cleared his throat. "Meet us at the station."

"I'm on the way."

"I'm coming, too," Lee said. "I'll drop the dogs with Sophie and fill her in. Then I can walk over."

Ellen frowned. "I don't know that's the safest thing to do."

He looked at Gerald. "I think the danger is past. He was the other one outside my window the other night."

"You're sure?"

"Yes, I recognize the voice. The other one was Freddie."

"And he's still on the loose."

He looked around. "I'll be fine."

She sighed. "I'll walk with you, then we can go over to the station together."

"Ellen—"

"Seriously. Until Freddie is caught, we have to watch each others' backs." She planned to watch his whether he liked it or not.

He gave a slow nod. "All right. Thanks."

Ellen explained to the chief that she'd be there shortly.

He drove off with a still-protesting Gerald in the backseat. Ellen sent a text to Sophie.

Had a situation at the vet's office. Need to leave the three goldens in your kennel right now. Is that all right?

Bring them on over, Sophie texted back.

The ambulance left with Tanya and the prison guard. Ellen turned the sign in the vet's window to Closed and drew in a deep breath. She set the clinic's door to lock behind her and pulled it shut. She and Lee walked the dogs to the training center and Sophie met them at the door. "What's going on? I saw all the chaos."

"Tanya's vet tech opened fire on her and his prison guard with a tranquilizer gun."

Sophie's eyes went wide. "What? Why?"

"We think it has to do with the puppies we're leaving with you, so make sure you set the alarm and don't open the door to anyone you don't know." She quickly explained what happened.

Sophie's eyes narrowed. "Do you need help with this?"

"No, we're on the way to the station to sit in on the interview with Chief Jones."

"All right, keep me posted."

"Will you update the others?"

"Of course."

Ellen and Lee left to walk the quarter of a mile to the police station. Ellen bounded up the steps and Lee followed close behind her. He reached around her to open the door for her and she raised a brow. "Thanks."

"Of course."

Once inside, Ellen found Carrie at the desk. Another

desk had been added next to Carrie's, and Missy seemed to be engrossed in whatever was on her computer screen. "Hi, Carrie, Missy," Ellen said. "Where's the chief?"

"In the interrogation room," Carrie said.

"Thanks. Could you do me a favor?"

"Sure, what do you need?"

"Could you get me everything you can find on Gerald Nees and then bring me the iPad with his info?"

"Of course."

Ellen paused. "Did the chief already ask for the information?"

Carrie looked at her over the top of her glasses. "No."

Ellen pursed her lips and nodded, then motioned for Lee to follow and headed down the hall. "You'll probably have to wait outside, but I promise I'll fill you in on what I can."

"What you can?"

She sighed. "Go through that door right there. You'll be able to see and hear everything that goes on in this room. The chief will probably be in there in a few minutes. If he doesn't kick you out, then you can stay."

He nodded. "That works."

She shot him a tight smile and knocked on the door. "It's Ellen, Chief."

Footsteps sounded then the door swung open. Chief Jones had a scowl the size of the Grand Canyon on his face. "You can take over for a bit. I'm about to send this guy into next week."

Ellen slipped her weapon from the holster on her hip and handed it to her boss. "Hold on to this for me, will you?"

He took it and she entered the room. The chief left and pulled the door shut behind him. She knew he'd be watching from the room next door. She figured Gerald knew it, too.

Gerald sat at a small rectangular table in a hard wooden chair. His hands were cuffed behind his back and his left foot shackled to the floor.

"You've got yourself into a bit of a mess, don't you?"

"Shut up." The sneer he'd left with still sat on his face.

"Well, that's certainly an option. I could shut up and just leave you here, but how is that going to help either of us?" He stared at her. She filtered her words. Considering and discarding at the speed of light. She had to say the right things. She walked over to the chair opposite him and sat. Then put her feet on the table. "You hungry?"

He blinked. "Yeah. Why?"

"Well, we're required to feed prisoners. What do you want?"

"What is this? Good cop, bad cop?"

Ellen made sure her facial expression didn't change. "Do you want something or not?"

"A hamburger all the way and fries."

She pulled her phone from the clip on her side and dialed the front desk. Carrie answered and Ellen placed the order. Carrie's silence echoed through the line. Then, "Ookay. Is it all right if I send Missy to pick it up?"

"Of course. I'll pay her back."

She hung up and Gerald stared at her. "Why'd you do that? I'm not talking to you."

She shrugged. "I know, but like I said, we're required to feed prisoners."

She sat there in silence, watching him. He shifted

under her gaze and wouldn't meet her eyes. Her phone buzzed and she looked at it. From the chief. What are you doing, Ellen?

Just let me play this out, she texted back.

Fine.

For the next twenty-five minutes, Ellen sat quietly while Gerald picked at his fingernail. Or shifted in his chair. Or spoke one sentence. "I'm not talking to you." When the food arrived, the chief brought it in and dropped it on the table in front of Ellen. His eyes met hers and she winked. He gave a minuscule shrug and didn't say a word as he walked back out the door and shut it once more.

Ellen pushed the food across the table in front of Gerald. He looked at it and licked his lips. She figured it had been a while since he had a good juicy hamburger. "I guess you need your hands."

"I guess." He still hadn't taken his eyes from the bag with the food.

"I'll uncuff you, but if you so much as twitch wrong, my boss will be in here within seconds, understand?"

"I'm not going to do anything." He sighed. He shook his leg and the chain clanked. "It's not like I'd be able to get very far. And besides, I want that burger."

She walked behind him and uncuffed his hands. He attacked the bag, had the hamburger unwrapped and a bite in his mouth faster than she could blink.

He swallowed and took another bite. "Good?"

"Yeah."

"Can you tell me why you're after the dogs?"

"Nope."

"Why?"

"Because I like breathing," he said with his mouth full.

"Do you know who killed Veronica Earnshaw?"

"The dog lady? I heard about that."

"Right, the dog lady." Ellen leaned forward.

"Nope. I don't know who killed her. Wasn't me, obviously." He smirked around another bite of the burger.

"Obviously. But you might have heard something."

"Hmm… No, not really. Just that she'd been killed."

Ellen bit down on her frustration. "Look, Gerald, you and I know that seeing those dogs set something off in you today or we wouldn't be sitting here. We've already checked the chips and one of them reads funny. We've figured out that it's a code for something, and it's only a matter of time before we crack it. You keep insisting you're not going to talk, but you could make things go a little easier on yourself if you would help us."

He froze. Then pushed the remnants of the burger away from him. "I want a lawyer."

And that was that.

Ellen leaned back, frustrated and satisfied all at the same time. "So it's a code. Thanks for that. I'll put the word out you helped us."

He shot to his feet. Ellen didn't blink, just stared up at him. "You can't do that!"

"Of course I can. You did help."

"I did not!"

"Well, everyone knows it's only the snitches who get the good food. Once it gets out that we're feeding you from the Cactus Café, who's going to believe you didn't give us some information in exchange for the hamburger and fries?"

With a howl of rage, he swept the table of the remains of his food and lunged at her. Ellen had expected his reaction and remained out of reach. The chain shackling him to the floor stretched and yanked him back. He landed with an awkward thump back in the chair. His chest heaved as he seethed and glared at her. She smiled. "Thanks, Gerald. I'll let the chief take over now and he can call your lawyer for you."

The door opened. Chief Jones met her eyes and she saw the respect shining there. They exchanged a small smile and Ellen slipped out the door.

THIRTEEN

"You really enjoyed that, didn't you?" Lee asked when she stepped into the hall.

"Oh, yes, that was fun. I just wish I could have gotten more out of him."

Lee took her hand. "You're a good cop, Ellen."

She looked surprised. "Thanks."

He frowned. "You still need to watch your back, though."

She echoed his frown. "I can take care of myself."

"Hmm. Right."

She sighed and let out a rueful laugh. "Except when inmates get their hands on a tranquilizer gun." Her eyes softened. "Thanks for that, by the way."

"Of course." He sighed. "He didn't know anything about Veronica's death."

"No, I don't think so. I think whatever's going on with the veterinary techs and the three puppies is something completely separate from Veronica's murder."

"So you don't think whoever is after the golden retriever puppies killed Veronica?" he asked.

"No, I wouldn't think so. She was microchipping the German shepherd puppies at the time of her death, and

I do think the one that she let escape may have information related to her killer. But I don't think the golden puppies and the code on Dash's chip connect to that. I think her death is something else entirely."

"I think you're right." He rubbed his eyes. "So this has originated from the prison."

"That's what I'm thinking. Whoever is behind this—and it could be Tanya even as it galls me to say it—is using the inmates. Having two crooked vet techs isn't a coincidence. I'm going to see if the chief will talk with Ken Bucks to see if he can get anything out of him if he's involved in this."

Lee snorted. "Ken's already given up what he's going to give up, I'm guessing. I really think that if we figure out what the numbers and letters mean on Dash's chip, we'll have a good idea why someone is so intent on stealing the dogs."

"I agree, but I'm going to recommend the chief do it anyway."

Lee nodded. "All right. In the meantime, I'm going back to the training center. We have that group of summer camp kids coming for their field trip."

"Good," she said. "We start our camps next month, full-blown all-day camps. You think we're ready?"

Lee gave her a slight smile. "Of course. We have a few more staff we need to hire, but I'm going through the résumés and pulling some I think will be good matches."

"Great."

He frowned. "We still have one problem for the moment, though."

"What's that?"

"Where to keep the golden puppies. I don't want to keep them at the center, not as long as Freddie is still on the loose and looking for them. I don't want to take a chance on putting the children in danger."

Ellen's eyes went wide. "You're absolutely right. We have to protect the people coming into the center." She bit her lip. "I don't have room at my house. Maybe Sophie—"

"I do."

"Your house?"

"I'm set up for it."

"But are you sure you want them there? Freddie's probably working for someone. The same someone who had him shoot at us and try to break in to your house, remember?"

"Yes. I mean, think about it. They've already come looking for the dogs once at my house. I'm guessing they might not come back."

"Maybe, but I sure wouldn't want to stake my life on it."

"I don't think it's a huge risk. I'm going to ask a friend to watch over the property and the dogs. If he sees anything suspicious, all he has to do is dial 911."

"Who are you thinking of?"

"I shared a cell with him for a year. He was released at the end of that year."

"And you trust him?"

"I do."

She shrugged. "All right, sounds good to me."

Lee nodded. "I'll call him from the training center and have him meet me there. He can take the dogs to the house and I can work with the kids. We've been rather absent from the center the past few days."

"Tell me about it," she muttered. "I'll find someone to

stay with you while you're at the center. Ryder or Tristan can probably do it."

He frowned. "I'll be fine."

"I know."

"But you're still going to ask someone to shadow me."

"Yep. I have a feeling the chief is going to ask me to ride with him to transport our prisoner to the prison. That's an hour's drive away. I don't want to leave you alone and unprotected while I'm out of town."

"I get that, but who's going to protect you?"

"Lee, I'm a trained police officer. Not only can I protect myself, I'll have the chief watching my back."

"And we've seen how efficient he is. You still bleed red just like anyone else," he snapped.

She stamped a foot. "Ooh, you are so frustrating sometimes. You still see me as that little high school girl who couldn't crawl out from beneath her mother's thumb. Well, I'm not that girl anymore and it's time you opened your eyes and saw that."

"Ellen, it's not that, I'm just—"

"You're just what, Lee? Concerned? Worried?"

"Yes," he snapped back. "Concerned and worried about a lot of things."

"Like what?"

"Like when your mother wakes up, she'll call the shots with you once again."

She blinked. "That was really random. Where did that come from?"

He swallowed. "I don't know."

"Well, you don't have to worry or be concerned about that, Lee. I'll be gone from Desert Valley so fast it'll make your head spin. I'll leave before I'll let that happen again."

Lee stepped forward and planted his lips on hers before he had a chance to think about what he was doing. It was a hard kiss—and maybe a bit desperate. When he lifted his head, he stared down into her shocked eyes. "Just something else for you to think about while you're thinking about leaving."

He spun on his heel, opened the door, stepped out of the room and let the door close with a quiet *snick*.

The perfect exit. A movie-scene-worthy exit.

And his heart was breaking with each step that took him farther and farther away from the woman he'd never stopped loving.

As she absently watched the chief make absolutely no headway with Gerald Nees, Ellen nursed her wounded heart and held her fingers over the lips Lee had just very thoroughly kissed. "You're not helping yourself here," the chief said.

"I'm not helping you, that's for sure," Nees shot back. "No matter what kind of food you give me."

Shortly after Lee's exit, Tristan had stuck his head in the observation room door and raised a brow. Ellen had shrugged and Tristan hadn't questioned the stormy atmosphere. He'd simply promised to keep an eye on Lee. She felt good about that. She and Lee had argued and said things she felt they both probably regretted. She didn't feel so good about that. Then he'd kissed her.

She was still feeling that. Good or bad didn't factor in. Just...wow.

While Carly snoozed in the corner, Chief Jones continued to wrangle with the stubborn prisoner. Ellen finally managed to shove Lee to the back of her mind. The more she watched the proceedings through the two-way mirror, the more she wanted to go through it, grab Gerald by his throat and give him a good shake in hopes something would jog loose and spill from his tongue.

The truth, a lie. She didn't care at this point. Just something. But he was tight-lipped and hard-eyed. "I have a good lawyer," he said. "I'm not saying anything until I talk to him. I can still beat this."

The chief laughed. An incredulous, "you're dumb as a rock" laugh. "You were caught red-handed. There are witnesses who saw what *you* did. Who are in the hospital recovering from the wounds *you* inflicted. What reality are you living in?"

Nees tightened his lips, locked his arms across his chest and fixed his stare on the table.

The chief finally stood and shook his head. "Fine. We'll get you transported to the prison, where you can wait to see the magistrate."

Gerald didn't look up.

Ellen met the chief in the hallway. He shut the door that locked from the outside and met her gaze. "Feel like taking a ride?"

"I thought you might ask."

He grimaced. "Sorry, but I'm not getting anything out of him."

She shrugged. "He's lawyered up anyway. It's fine."

"Let me just call the prison to let them know we're headed that way."

While the chief made the call, Ellen took Carly into the woods at the back of the station. She dug a ball out of her bag and gave it a toss. Carly took off like a shot to snag it and bring it back to her. For the next five minutes, she threw and Carly fetched.

When the chief waved to her from the back door, she

whistled for the dog and they headed inside. "You get it all arranged?" she asked.

"Yep. Let's go."

She followed him to the room where Gerald Nees still sat. "Ready to ride?"

"Whatever."

"Your lawyer's meeting you there."

Gerald's glare never lessened. Chief Jones led him to the DVPD SUV he drove and opened the door. He helped Gerald get in and made sure his seat belt was fastened and his hands were secured so that he wouldn't be able to reach into the front seat at any time. Ellen opened the passenger's front door and motioned for Carly to get in. The dog did. "I wouldn't normally put her up front, Chief, but I don't want her in the back with this guy." She glared at the perp.

Ellen climbed into the backseat behind the dog and waited for Chief Jones to heft himself behind the wheel.

"Keep an eye out, Chief," she murmured. "My nerves are twitching."

He shot her a glance in the rearview mirror. "Okay. I'll be watching the mirrors."

She nodded, checked once more to make sure Gerald's hands were bound securely and unclipped the strap over her weapon. It would be an hour there plus time to process Gerald and then an hour back. She'd be home shortly after the training center closed. The argument with Lee played in her mind and she winced. She owed him an apology. Another one.

She pulled her phone from her pocket and sent Lee a text. Meet me at the training center around six? I owe you an apology. I'll order delivery. We'll eat and discuss the plans for the camp. If you already have something and can't make it, we'll just get together tomorrow.

She slipped the phone back onto her belt and glanced in the rearview mirror. "You really think Freddie has the guts to try something?"

Chief Jones grunted. "I don't know about Freddie. Maybe whoever he's working with."

"Maybe. It bothers me that Gerald thinks this is going to go away. Like there's someone who can take care of it and *will*."

The chief shook his head and started the vehicle. He pulled out of the parking lot and Ellen sent up a prayer for everyone's safety. When the chief pulled past the training center, she noticed Tristan's, Shane's and Ryder's vehicles out front. "Did you call in reinforcements, too?" she asked.

"I did."

"Excellent."

"They'll follow Lee home and keep an eye on things there, as well."

With that much police coverage on the puppies and Lee, Ellen felt like she could relax a bit. The goldens were safe at Lee's home also with protection. All should be well.

Should be.

Except why did she still feel the pinch of apprehension? Like the other shoe was going to drop, and if she didn't duck fast enough, it was going to land on her head?

She sighed and watched the scenery pass by, all the while watching the mirrors. So far so good.

She prayed it stayed that way.

Because a killer that was still at large and possibly looking for the next victim.

FOURTEEN

Lee clapped the nine-year-old on the shoulder and high-fived him. "Great job, Henry. I think you have a future in dog training if you want it." Lee picked up Dancer and held the animal in the crook of his arm.

Henry flushed his pleasure and stroked the silky dog's ears. Lee looked up and caught the teacher's eye. She'd explained that she'd set up this field trip specifically for Henry, a child who'd come from an abusive background and refused to speak. He was currently in foster care and was up for adoption. The family he was with had already filled out the paperwork, and gone through the extensive process to make him a part of their family. Everything would be final next week.

"I think a therapy dog would be great for Henry," Mrs. Ivan had said on the phone the first day Lee had been on the job. She was a sharp woman in her early fifties who obviously loved her students and went above and beyond the call of duty by volunteering to teach summer school—referred to as summer camp by her and her students. "His parents have given the green light, so maybe you could see if you have a dog to pair with him?"

"I think I have the perfect dog. We'll need Henry's parents to come in and give the final seal of approval."

"Of course. I think the other children will benefit from seeing your program in action, so the field trip will be good for all."

Now it was time for the small class to leave. Henry slipped his small hand into Lee's and looked up at him. Though he didn't move his lips, his eyes spoke for him. Lee lightly squeezed the boy's small fingers. "You're welcome."

Henry smiled, looked longingly at Dancer, the black cocker spaniel he'd bonded with almost instantly. He reached out for one more scratch behind the ears and Dancer licked his fingers. A giggle escaped and Lee heard Mrs. Ivan smother a light gasp. He met her eyes and saw the joy there. Henry reluctantly moved to get in the line in front of his teacher.

"We have time for one more question," Mrs. Ivan said. Three hands shot up and Lee pointed to a cute girl with Down syndrome and blond pigtails.

"Yes, ma'am," he said.

She giggled. "I'm not a ma'am."

"What's your question, Tabitha?" Mrs. Ivan prompted.

"Where do these dogs come from? Were they all borned here? In America?"

The teacher cleared her throat. "Born."

"Yes." Tabitha nodded. "Born."

Lee, still holding Dancer, moved to the wall map and pointed to North America. "Okay, kids. What's this piece of paper here?"

Several children chuckled. "A map!" Several voices overlapped.

"Exactly. You guys are smart." More giggles. "Now

even though this training center has only been open for a short time, we have several dogs that came from Texas. Can anyone find Texas?"

All hands went up. Lee picked the nearest gap-toothed boy. "Show us." The nine-year-old went to the map and pointed to the correct state. "Excellent," Lee said. "Now we also have several that came from New Mexico, Utah and Nevada. Can you show me those states?"

"I can."

And so it went until the teacher nodded to Lee. "And that's it kids," he said. "Thanks for coming by today. The animals loved it and I hope you did, too."

Cheers and claps erupted and he smiled. Henry held his gaze for another moment then walked out the door, last in line, in no hurry to leave.

Lee waved. Henry spun on his heel and ran back to Dancer. Lee bent down and Henry kissed the dog on her head. "She'll be waiting for you, Henry."

Another smile lifted the child's lips and he ran back just in time to slip through the door and join his class.

Lee glanced at his watch and wondered how Ellen was doing. Then he looked at his phone and read her text. Six o'clock at the training center. To discuss plans for the camp? He sighed and rubbed his face. He wanted to talk about more than plans for the camp but wasn't sure how receptive Ellen would be to the idea. He knew he was her employee; he respected her position and knew that if he pushed things romantically, it could muddy the waters.

But he'd been crazy about her in high school and he'd never forgotten her. Now a second chance with her might be staring him in the face. If he didn't grab hold of it with both hands, he could lose her forever. His heart shuddered at the thought yet indecision gripped him. She'd already broken his heart once. Did he want to put himself in the position that would allow her to do it again? He glanced at his watch then rubbed his eyes.

The door pinged and automatically opened. A young man in his early thirties, seated in a wheelchair, rolled himself through. Lee straightened. "Hi. Can I help you?"

Hard blue eyes met his. "I heard about this place. Heard I could get a service dog to help me out."

"I'm sure we could work something out. I'm Lee Earnshaw."

"I'm Travis Lyons."

Lee shook the man's hand and noticed the callouses. "What happened to put you in the chair?"

"Took a bullet to the spine, thanks to my best friend. He decided I wasn't good enough for his sister and—" he shrugged, but Lee could see the anger beneath the surface "—he took it upon himself to see that I wasn't. Doc says I'm going to be in this chair for the rest of my life and I need to come to terms with it. Suggested I check this place out."

"Well, we're about to close, but I don't mind giving you a quick tour."

The eyes thawed slightly. "That'd be great. Thanks." He jerked a thumb toward the door he'd just rolled through. "You have an awful lot of security around here."

"Yeah. There's a reason for it, but don't worry, those guys are good. As long as they're out there, we're fine in here."

Travis nodded and gave another shrug. "Good to know."

Lee led the way through the facility, his mind only partially on the tour. He couldn't push Ellen from his thoughts. She continued the invasion all the way through the tour. The last stop was the kennel. "This is where we keep the dogs while we're training them."

"Cool." He rolled past one kennel, then the next and the next. Finally, he spun to face Lee, his expression hard. "I like dogs. I don't like the reason I need one."

"I understand."

"Yeah." He looked away a minute, then back at Lee. "All right. I'll be in touch."

"Want to schedule an appointment? We'll do an interview, see what kind of dog would match best with your personality."

"I'll call you. I've got some thinking to do. You got a bathroom I can use before I go?"

"Of course." He pointed. "Just down that hall and to the left. You…ah…need any help or anything?" As soon as the words left his lips, he flushed. "Sorry, I guess I need to brush up on my wheelchair etiquette."

Travis flashed a grin, the first sign of something other than hard anger in his eyes. "Naw, man, I'm good." He rolled down the hall and disappeared into the bathroom. While Lee waited for Travis, he finished doing some of the daily closing chores. When he took the trash out, he noticed the door-open sign on the alarm system panel. "Weird," he muttered. He came back in to find Travis in the lobby heading for the door.

"Thanks again for your help."

"Sure. See you soon." He showed the man out and watched him roll toward the gray van parked in the handicapped spot near the front of the building. Lee shook his head. Okay, he had to admit, his own problems seemed minimal in light of Travis's.

"Have a good night, Lee."

He looked up to see one of the other workers headed for the door. "You too, Miranda."

"The dogs have all eaten. I also cleaned all the kennels and put fresh water in the bowls, so they should be good for the night."

"What would we do without you?"

"Scoop a lot more poop?"

He laughed, his weariness fading a bit with her teasing. "That's for sure. See you tomorrow."

Miranda left and Lee looked around to see if he needed to do anything else before locking up—or planting himself in the office to wait for Ellen.

The door. He walked to the back to check on the door indicated on the panel and found it shut. He checked the panel again and saw that it was fine. He frowned and made a mental note to mention it to Ellen. Could be a glitch in the system. He glanced in each room as he passed, checked the dogs one more time and pondered what his next move would be. Stay? Or go?

The people who'd broken in and attacked the guard were after the puppies. Now that the puppies were no longer at the facility, the problem should go away. Or at least be transferred to Lee's property.

And with all of the rookies, along with the rest of those on the force, taking turns watching his place in pairs, he didn't think the intruders wouldn't be back. But he felt sure they were watching for the next opportunity to grab the golden retriever puppies should it present itself. He didn't intend for that to happen.

His mind circled back to the problem at hand. Stay and eat with Ellen or go home and lick his wounds? He sighed. He'd enjoyed the field trip today. And seeing Henry's eyes light up had made his week. He thought about his plans to finish up school and become a veterinarian. It seemed as though something was always getting in the way and slowing him down.

Like his feelings for Ellen.

He walked over to the desk and grabbed his keys. His eyes fell on the map and he smiled. The kids had their geography down pat.

He froze.

Wait a minute.

Geography.

Something niggled at the back of his mind.

He frowned. What was it? He continued to ponder what was trying to come to the forefront of his brain, but he couldn't quite grasp it. But it had to do with the map. He sighed and shook his head. Maybe if he didn't think so hard, it would come to him.

He looked at his phone.

Dinner with Ellen or go home?

Heartbreak or play it safe?

He turned on the alarm and locked the door behind him.

Ellen was tired. Gerald and his lawyer had clammed up and Chief Jones had stalked out, muttering under his breath about retirement looking better and better every day.

Within minutes, they were on the road and on the way back to Desert Valley. Ellen's senses were alert but she was glad to have made it to the prison without incident. She'd been tight and tense the whole drive, sure someone would follow them to try to help Gerald escape. But all had gone well, and now it was time to get back and hash out a plan with Lee. If he was up to dinner. Her pulse picked up speed at the thought of spending time with him, being in the same space as him. "It's just business," she whispered. "Just business."

"You say something?"

She jumped. "Oh, talking to myself, Chief. Sorry."

He eyed her for a second then turned his attention back to the road. "Thanks for riding out here with me. I wouldn't have put it past the guy to have someone watching us."

"I know. But nothing happened. Which makes me nervous."

"How so?"

"Gerald is obviously a part of some ring. Those numbers on that chip mean something."

"I know, I agree."

She glanced at her phone. Still no reply from Lee.

"You expecting an important call?"

"No, I just left a message for Lee to call me, but he hasn't." She dialed his number and listened to it ring. Four times then voice mail. "Hey, Lee, can you give me a call? You haven't answered my text and you're not answering your phone. I'm getting a little worried. Please call me back." She hung up.

Chief Jones shook his head. "That was a raw deal Lee Earnshaw got with Ken framing him. I'm ashamed that man was even a part of my force—or my family." Ken Bucks was the chief's stepson.

"I agree. It was an incredibly raw deal, but Lee's handling it well." She considered calling Shane or Tristan but knew if something was really wrong, one or both of them would be in contact.

Which meant that Lee didn't have his phone on him

and hadn't seen that she was trying to get in touch with him.

Or he was ignoring her, and that stung.

She bit her lip and checked the mirrors, then the time.

She'd arrive back at the training center about ten minutes before six. She texted, Do I pick up dinner or not?

Almost instantly her phone dinged a response.

Not tonight, thanks. We'll talk tomorrow.

FIFTEEN

Ellen stepped into the training center, and the chief took off for home. Eddie Harmon sat outside and waved as she shut the door behind her. She stood in the dark lobby for a few moments, taking in the smells and the fact that she had done something good. Something that helped others. That part felt amazing, but the fact that she had no one to share it with created an emptiness inside her. She fought the urge to shed a few tears and ignored the stinging in her heart while she checked on the dogs. They were all excited to see her, and she stopped by each kennel to scratch ears and offer words of praise and love. Carly padded at her side casting anxious glances her way as though she could sense the turmoil raging inside her master.

Ellen made her way into the office, dropped some bags of food on the desk and plopped into her chair. Lee wasn't here. He really wasn't. Why she was so surprised she couldn't put her finger on, but she was. Even though he'd said he wasn't coming by, she knew she'd subconsciously expected him to be there.

Just like when she'd graduated from high school, she'd looked out into the audience, looking for her father. He hadn't been there. She'd spotted her mother, smiling brightly, but her dad had been nowhere to be seen. She remembered the heartbreak and realized the emotion she felt now mirrored that on her graduation day. She'd let her defenses down and, in a matter of days, Lee had slipped right back into her heart. Who was she kidding? He'd done that years ago and had been there ever since. Now what was she going to do?

Carly laid her head on Ellen's thigh and sighed. Ellen couldn't help it. One tear escaped and then another until she had a river flowing. She rested her forehead on her arms and gave in to it. The stress of her mother's medical condition and the fact that her attacker still roamed free, the emotional roller coaster her relationship—or the lack thereof—with Lee had her on and the indecision of whether to make a life in Desert Valley or follow through with her plans to leave once her mother was awake and Veronica's killer was caught. A silly thing to cry over, maybe, but she knew she needed the release. Then again, calling her life decisions "silly" wasn't right, either. They weren't silly; they were things she needed to deal with. She definitely deserved the cry.

Finally she sniffed, grabbed a tissue and cleaned herself up. "Okay, Carly, pity party's over."

Carly cocked her head then stood on her hind legs to swipe Ellen's face with her pink tongue. Ellen let out a shaky laugh and scratched the dog's silky ears. "I just wish God would send me an email, you know? Subject line reading, 'What to do with your life.'" She sighed. "Then again, maybe He's already sent his emails in the form of His word, eh, girl?" Carly sat on the floor.

A low thud from the back of the building had Ellen's nerves shivering. Carly popped to her feet and spun toward the door. Her ears swiveled and a low growl rumbled in her chest. Ellen rose to her feet, listening. "What do you think it is, girl?" Had Lee come back after all? She walked to the door. But if it was Lee, why was Carly's fur standing on end?

Ellen pulled her weapon and moved to the door. "Lee? That you?"

She listened.

Silence.

A footfall in the hallway.

Her stomach clenched. Her heart thudded a faster beat. She gripped her weapon and stepped out of the office, Carly at her side attached to her leash. She didn't need Carly bolting into a situation that would get her killed.

Senses sharpened by her surging adrenaline, she headed down the narrow hall toward the kennels. "The puppies aren't here!"

Silence. A stillness invaded the building and yet the air felt electrified, raising the hair on her arms and at the back of her neck. She placed one foot in front of the other.

When she came to the storage room, she tested the knob with her left hand. Locked. She kept going. Carly stayed with her, her nose quivering, ears twitching. Should she send the dog ahead? But if the person had a weapon...

Ellen kept Carly near and continued her search. Call it in? Or not?

Better safe than sorry.

She reached for her phone when she heard the soft *snick* of a door closing.

* * *

It was six thirty. Maybe he wasn't too late. He dialed Ellen's number again and it rang twice before transferring to her voice mail. Weird. He texted her. I'm on my way to the center. You're right, we need to talk. I think I know what the odd code on Dash's chip is.

Lee rubbed his eyes and shoved his key into the ignition. He was a jerk. She'd said she owed him an apology. He could have at least had dinner with her. He called again, and again got her voice mail. Shane waved at him and Lee lowered his window. "I'm sorry, but I'm going in to the assistance center."

"Now?"

"Yes, I need to clear something up with Ellen and she's not answering her phone. She left me a message saying she'd be at the assistance center so I'm going to go check on her."

"All right. It's fine. I'll follow you. Tristan will stay here with the guy you've got watching the dogs."

"Thanks." Lee started back to the Jeep with the thought that he really needed to check on the progress of his truck's repairs when he turned around and walked back to Shane. "I think I know what the code is on Dash's chip."

Shane lifted a brow. "What?"

"We had kids in on a field trip today and we were looking at the map and—" He waved a hand as though to push aside the explanation. "I think it's longitude and latitude running together. Or vice versa. I think it's a spot, a location."

Shane nodded. "Can't hurt to check it out. I'll call Ryder and see if he can put the numbers in and see what pops out."

"Great." He climbed into the Jeep and tried Ellen again one more time. When she still didn't pick up, he frowned. Now he was worried. He sent her yet another text. I'm heading your way. Let me know if you're still at the center and want me to pick up some food.

He pulled out of his drive and headed toward the main street of the town. He and Ellen needed to have a heart-to-heart chat, and now was as good a time as any. Avoiding the situation was only going to make him lose sleep, and he was fed up with that.

Shane's truck stayed with him about two car lengths behind. He liked having someone watching his back. He liked the security. He would like it even more if Ellen would listen to what he had to say.

Being in prison had taught him a lot of things. One of those was that life was unpredictable, that God was faithful no matter the circumstances or if it looked as though all was lost. And that he didn't want to be alone the rest of his life.

But it wasn't just that he didn't want to be alone, he wanted to have that special someone by his side. A woman he loved, who loved him in return. A teammate. Someone who would just do life with him. Maybe have a few kids. He swallowed at the thought. What kind of father would he be? His knuckles turned white on the wheel as he made a left onto the road that would take him to the center. He wouldn't be anything like his own father, that was for sure. As long as he did the opposite of what his dad had done, Lee was sure to be a great dad.

Maybe.

He just had to make sure Ellen felt the same way. He had no doubt he'd hurt her feelings tonight. Maybe she was giving him a taste of his own medicine and ignoring

his attempts to reach her. He grimaced. No, she wouldn't
do that. So why wasn't she answering? She was probably
working with a dog in order to take her mind off the fact
that he'd been a jerk to her.

Well, he was done with his momentary lapse into
immaturity.

So, ready or not, he was going to spill his heart out
to her and see what she said. If she sent him packing, so
be it. He'd find a way to live through it, but he wasn't
going to go through life with regrets.

Now if she'd just answer the phone.

Ellen glanced into the break room to her right. The
overhead lights were off, but the small night-light in the
socket next to the counter allowed her to see into the
room. All seemed well. Carly stayed silent, but pressed
against Ellen's leg. The dog had definitely picked up on
her tension and had been alerted to the fact that someone
was in the building. Or if it wasn't a person, *something*
had gotten her attention.

With one hand holding her weapon, she looped Carly's leash over her wrist and reached for her phone. It
buzzed against her hand. She glanced at the screen. Lee.

A scuffing sound behind her brought her head up
and around before she had a chance to respond. "Who's
there?"

Had she armed the alarm when she'd entered? Of
course she had. So who could possibly be inside? Only
someone with the code. The new code she'd programmed
the system with after the last break-in.

She frowned. Why would someone come back here?
The dogs weren't here, so what would be the purpose
in breaking back in to the center? Of course, the person

wouldn't know the dogs weren't at the center, so maybe he'd come back to try again? Her adrenaline rushed.

Ellen pressed the button to answer Lee's call only to find he'd already hung up. Instead of calling him back, she pressed the number for Dispatch. It was time for backup. The dispatcher answered on the second ring. Ellen held the phone to her ear. "Need backup at the Desert Valley Assistance Center," she whispered. Carly growled and tried to lunge forward, pulling her hand with the phone. Ellen lifted her arm so the leash couldn't slip over her wrist. "Carly, no." The dog reluctantly settled. Back into the phone, Ellen whispered, "There's definitely an intruder in the building. Need assistance ASAP."

"I have a unit on the way."

"Thanks."

Carly's hackles were raised, her attention on something at the end of the hall. The kennel? Were the dogs in danger? She shoved the phone into her pocket, still connected to the dispatcher, but she needed both hands. She gripped her weapon in her right hand and Carly's leash in the other. She moved cautiously in the direction Carly's attention was so focused on and stopped just before the door that led to the kennel area. She hadn't locked it after she'd checked on the dogs earlier because she'd planned to go back in one last time before leaving for the night. Pushing a silent breath through barely parted lips, she glanced through the glass window.

The kennel's lights were muted, but she could see well enough. The dogs didn't seem disturbed. They were quiet except for the couple that barked just because they were dogs and that was what they did. The barks weren't frantic or upset or angry.

Nothing that said "intruder." From her position near the window, all looked clear inside the area. She pressed the handle that would open the door. Carly growled and lunged at the door behind her. Ellen spun to see the craft room door cracked. She let the dog go. Carly bolted into the other room. Ellen heard a hissing sound, then Carly's yelp.

"Carly!" What had happened? Where was her backup? She moved toward the door, weapon outstretched. She shoved her back up against the wall. "Come on out! That room's a dead end. No way out!"

And the door was flung open. Her finger tightened on the trigger, but she couldn't see who to shoot at. Then something misted in her face. She gasped. Smelled a sickeningly sweet odor and tried to turn away from it.

She felt dizzy.

Her muscles went slack. Weak.

She heard her gun hit the floor.

Then she felt someone catch her.

The darkness wanted to close in, but she fought it. She turned her head. Saw Carly on the floor, not moving.

Drugged. Someone had sprayed them with something.

Then she felt herself being dragged.

Heard the sirens approaching.

And then knew nothing more.

SIXTEEN

Lee arrived just as the swarm of officers pulled into the parking lot. He jumped out of the Jeep and hurried toward the building.

"Police! Freeze!"

Lee spun, his hands in the air.

Shane got out of his vehicle and waved the others down. "He's good! He's with me." His German shepherd, Bella, stayed at his side.

"What's going on?" Lee shouted.

"Ellen called for backup," Ryder said. "Get back in the Jeep and stay there," he said to Lee.

Lee's fingers curled into fists. What was going on? Why would Ellen need backup? "Where is she?"

"That's what we're going to find out. Stay put."

"Ryder, come on, tell me what you know."

"She reported an intruder and asked for backup. Get back in the Jeep now!" Ryder and his partner, Titus, headed into the building.

Lee did as ordered, his heart in his throat as he watched the officers stop at the glass door. Ryder tried it and it was locked. He came back to Lee. "You have the key?"

Lee handed him the card to swipe. Within seconds, Ryder was back at the door. He swiped the card and Lee watched them stream inside one behind the other, weapons ready.

An intruder? Lee's gut clenched and he slammed a fist against the wheel as he watched law enforcement once again take over Ellen's business. Officers on the outside kept watch on the trees and the wooded area behind the building. Guilt swamped him. He should have been here. If he hadn't been so prideful, so worried about getting his heart broken—had he stayed, maybe he could have helped her.

He closed his eyes. *Please, God, give me another chance. I know I've used up a lot of them, but I don't care what chance I'm on, don't let anything happen to her. No matter what she decides, whether to stay or go, I need her to be okay. Please.* He didn't know how long he prayed, but it felt as though an eternity passed before the tap on his window jerked his eyes open.

Ryder. The tension around the man's mouth didn't bode well. Lee opened the door and climbed out. "What is it? What'd you find?"

"The building's been cleared. Carly's down and Ellen's missing."

Lee swayed. Caught himself on the door. "Carly? Down? Ellen's missing?"

"Carly's alive, but unconscious. No visible trauma. We're getting her over to the vet now. Tanya's in the hospital, but we have another one coming from a nearby town. He said he'd be here in twenty minutes."

"Good. What about Ellen?"

He nodded to the back of the building. "Her SUV is parked near the back entrance, but there's no sign of her."

"How did someone get in? The front door was locked. What about the back?"

"Locked and the alarm was turned off. Shane's pulling up video footage as we speak."

"Ellen would have had to turn the alarm off to enter the building, but she would have armed it once she was inside."

Ryder rubbed his jaw. "She could have forgotten. You sure?"

"Yes, I'm sure." And he was. "With all the crazy stuff going on around here lately, she wouldn't have taken any chances."

Ryder nodded. "I'm inclined to agree. So whoever was inside knows the code."

Chief Jones pulled up and climbed from his cruiser. "What's going on? I heard something about Ellen going missing."

Ryder filled him in while Lee continued to send up prayers and began to pace, thinking.

Chief Jones blew out a breath. "All right, who's searching for her?"

"James and Hawk are looking for her trail right now."

"Good. Let me know if they pick up her scent. In the meantime, we got a hit on the DNA on that glove used in the bank robbery."

Lee couldn't believe his ears. "Why are you worried about the bank robbery when Ellen's missing?"

"Because there's a connection."

"What kind of connection, Chief?"

"The DNA didn't match anyone in the system, but the lab tech ran the markers. There was a ninety-nine percent match to someone who *is* in the system."

"To who?" Lee asked.

"To the brother of the man who used to be Freddie Parrish's cell mate in prison. A long-time career criminal."

"What's his name?"

"Trevor Little. Here's his picture." Chief Jones held up his phone.

Lee leaned in and gasped. "He was here this afternoon. At the center."

"What?" Ryder, Shane and the chief echoed the question.

"He came in a wheelchair and he said his name was Travis Lyons." He ran a hand through his hair, his nerves standing on end. "I gave him a tour of the facility. He said he took a bullet to the spine and he was paralyzed…" Anger boiled. "Is he even in a wheelchair?"

"No. I'm guessing you were played and he was just casing the place."

"But he left. He wheeled out and got into his van and left. He may have cased the place, but that still doesn't explain how he got in after-hours and with the alarm set."

"Did you leave him alone at any time?" Ryder asked.

"No, I gave him the tour and he—" Lee froze.

"He what, Lee?" the chief pressed.

"He went to the bathroom. Just before he left. He was alone then." He pressed the heels of his hands to his eyes. "And shortly after he left, I noticed the alarm system said there was a door ajar. When I checked, I didn't find anything wrong and the alarm system went back to normal. I just figured it was a glitch and made a notation for Ellen to have it checked."

"He propped it open," Shane said. "Circled around and slipped back inside. Probably had someone else in the van to drive off after he was back in the building. He was already inside when Ellen came back."

Sickness swept over Lee. "It's my fault," he said. "I didn't do a thorough check of the building. I should have been more concerned about the signal on the panel." He pinched the bridge of his nose. If anything happened to Ellen…

"It's not your fault, Lee."

"We have to find her."

James and Hawk, the bloodhound who could sniff out just about anything, returned from the trees bordering the property. "What did you find?" the chief asked.

James trotted over and, with a huff, Hawk flopped onto the ground next to him. "Hawk had the trail up through the woods and out the other side. It leads to the road. He had a car waiting."

"How did he get her there?"

"Had to carry her."

"Which means he's strong."

"The guy who came in," Lee said, "his upper arms were well muscled. Ripped. Like he worked out a lot. He wouldn't have any trouble carrying her."

"Or rolling her," Shane said.

"What do you mean?"

He held out an iPad. "Check out the video footage."

Lee leaned forward and watched the black-and-white film. The outside front cameras showed the man Lee knew as Travis leaving in his van. When Shane switched to the back cameras, it showed him coming though the woods toward the building pushing a wheelchair.

And then he was inside the building, leaving the wheelchair outside next to the door.

"What about the cameras inside?" Lee asked softly.

Shane tapped the screen and brought up another view forwarded by about an hour. "There. He was hiding in the back room across from the kennel area."

"That's the kids' craft room," Lee said.

Ellen came on-screen with Carly at her side. They watched her check the kennel door then saw Carly lunge at the craft room and Ellen let her go.

Then Ellen had her weapon held in front of her as she moved to the door. Then she jerked back, brought a hand to her face and stumbled.

"What did he hit her with?"

"He sprayed her with something."

"It knocked her out pretty fast. Chloroform?"

"Maybe."

Lee watched Ellen wobble, try to regain her footing. The craft room door opened, and the guy caught Ellen as she started to sink to the floor. He gathered her up and pushed out the back door.

Another quick tap on the screen took him back to the outdoor camera. "And here they come. He puts her in the wheelchair and off they go," Shane said. "Smart, not carrying her out. No one would give it a second thought if he was seen rolling her in a wheelchair."

Lee felt sick. "Yeah, if he was carrying her…"

"Yeah," Shane said.

"But why would they come after her? I thought it was the dog they wanted. Why Ellen?"

"She has something they want?"

"What?"

"Like you said, they want the dog," Shane said.

"But she doesn't have the dog, I do."

Shane blew out a slow breath. "Everyone, stay close to your phone."

* * *

Ellen opened her eyes and blinked. Then immediately shut them. Pain, nausea, dry mouth. Dizziness. Even in her prone position, her head was spinning. What was *wrong* with her? The flu? Had she passed out?

She kept her eyes closed and waited for the dizziness and nausea to pass. While she waited, she forced herself to think. Carly. Her eyes flew open and she stared at a white ceiling. A single bulb stared back at her. That was not her bedroom ceiling in her mother's home.

What had happened? How had she gotten here?

She moved her fingers. And gasped. Her hands were bound in front of her and the tape was tight. She felt a rough blanket beneath her. She was on a cot. A hard one. Her stomach rumbled. She was hungry in spite of the queasiness in her belly. Maybe hunger was part of the queasiness. *Think, Ellen.* She had a flash of being in the center, Carly at her side with her gun drawn.

Her gun.

She moved her hands to her right hip. Felt her holster. Empty.

Panic threatened. Why couldn't she remember?

Where was she?

And why were her hands bound?

She rolled to her side and groaned. The room shifted, her nausea intensified. She closed her eyes again and stayed as still as possible. And while her body remained motionless, her mind spun.

She'd been at the center. She'd had her gun drawn. She remembered Carly's growling and lunging at the door then…

…nothing.

Okay, she'd have to remember later. Right now she needed to get out of here.

Wherever *here* was.

She had to move. The nausea had subsided with her stillness and she was loath to do anything to bring it back.

But...

Ellen took a breath and slowly raised her upper body, letting her legs fall off the cot.

The room whirled; the sickness returned. She stayed still. Found a spot on the far cement wall and locked her gaze on it. She wasn't sure how long she sat, but finally everything seemed to settle. Her stomach, her head. She dared let her eyes move from the spot on the wall.

It was a large room. Cement walls, white ceiling. Metal rails on the ceiling. No windows. "Of course not. That would be too easy, wouldn't it?" Her muttered words echoed around her.

Slowly, oh, so slowly, she slid from the cot and stood on shaky legs, careful because if she fell, it would be next to impossible to break the fall. Okay, she was feeling better. Why was she here? What did the person who'd snatched her want?

She'd been at the center. She'd been sad that Lee wasn't going to be joining her for dinner. And then she'd heard a noise. Or rather Carly had. Right, she remembered all that.

And Lee...poor Lee. Did he know what had happened? She swallowed—or tried to. Her throat was so dry. "Lee, I'm sorry," she whispered. "I'm sorry."

When he found out she was missing, he would blame himself. She couldn't let that happen. Fear shivered through her and a desperation to live, to find out what her future held. And make sure Lee was a part of that future. She knew that she wasn't supposed to live though this. She was simply a pawn in these people's deadly game. When they finished with her, got what they wanted, they'd toss her aside like yesterday's trash. If she was going to survive, she was going to have to get away.

Time to explore her surroundings.

And figure out how to get out before whoever put her here came back.

SEVENTEEN

Lee thought his head might explode. No one had a lead on Ellen's whereabouts. The only thing that made him feel slightly better was that Carly was now fine and sitting in the back of Shane's vehicle along with Shane's dog, Bella. The consensus was that Carly and Ellen had both been sprayed with the same substance. Other than being very thirsty, the fact that Carly had bounced back so fast was reassuring.

That Ellen was still missing was not.

He walked over to Chief Jones, James and Hawk. "What's next?" His phone rang before anyone could answer him. He snatched it off his belt clip and slapped it to his ear without even looking at the screen. "Ellen?"

"You have the golden retriever puppies?"

Lee froze. "You're not Ellen."

"No. I'm not. But I know where she is. You have the puppies?"

"Yes." Lee motioned to the chief and the others and pointed to his phone.

"Put it on speaker," James hissed.

Chief Jones motioned for everyone to be quiet. The noise level died down.

Lee pressed the button. The man's voice floated into the night air. "…you want to see Ellen again, I want the puppy, the small one, in my possession within the hour."

"Where do I bring him?"

"I'll text you. And don't try tracing this phone. I'll save you the trouble. It's a burner. And I'm going to toss it as soon as we hang up. The text will come from a different number."

"How do I know Ellen's alive?"

"Because as long as you're bringing me the puppy, I have no reason to kill her."

"I'll bring it. But I want proof Ellen is alive."

"You'll just have to trust me. And leave the cops out of it."

Lee winced and met Chief Jones's eyes. Too late for that. "So you're going to trade me Ellen for the puppy?"

"Yes. As long as you follow my instructions, you'll get the cop back in one piece."

"Fine. What are your instructions?"

"In a few minutes, I'm going to text you an address. You come to that address with the puppy only, and you might get your girlfriend back."

"I need some proof she's alive."

Silence fell on the other end. Then his phone dinged. "There's your proof. Now, when you get the address, be there within the hour. If I see even a hint of the police, I'll kill her. You understand?"

Fear clenched Lee's throat. The man was serious. His tone was no-nonsense. "Yes, I understand."

"Good."

"What about—" But he was talking to dead air. Lee pressed the button to pull up the picture he'd been sent.

He gasped.

Ellen lay on a cot, her eyes closed, hands bound in front of her. She looked so pale and still. And small. Everything in him raged that someone would do this to her. He looked up into the chief's eyes. "Not getting her back is not an option." And he was going to do everything in his power to help, because the first thing he was going to tell her when he held her again was how much he loved her.

Ellen examined every square inch of the large room, desperate to find anything that she might be able to use to facilitate her escape. She had to get her hands loose. They were tingling and soon would be numb. She opened and closed her fingers. What could she use to cut through the tape? Her teeth hadn't done much good.

She looked around again, this time focusing on the walls. She needed something sharp. A nail. Anything. The room had been a garage once upon a time. No doubt about it. But it had been closed in and cleaned out. The door had two deadbolt locks. One that locked from the inside and one from the outside. She wasn't getting out the door.

Originally she'd thought there weren't any windows, but upon closer inspection, she saw they'd just been boarded up and painted over to match the walls. If she could get one of the pieces of plywood loose, she might have a chance to get out. The bottom of the window came to the top of her head. She'd broken three nails trying to pull the wood off and quickly figured out that wasn't going to work. Her hands simply weren't strong enough.

Thankfully her head had quit spinning and her muscles were starting to feel stronger again.

She stood at the center of the room flexing her fingers. A table leaned against the back wall. An old chair sat in the corner. No toolbox, of course.

A scrape just outside the door sent her running for the cot. She lay on her side, positioning herself so she could kick out in a smooth move. Assuming her kidnapper got that close.

The lock snicked and the door opened. She cracked her eyes and saw a man shut the door behind him. And lock it with the key. He slid the key into the front pocket of his jeans. Her heart thudded. Self-defense moves came to mind, but if she managed to knock him down and get to the door, she couldn't get out without the key. And with her hands still tightly taped, she was fairly helpless.

On a positive note, he didn't seem to have a weapon on him. Which might mean he was pretty confident that he didn't need one.

"I know you're awake."

His voice rumbled through the garage. She didn't try to keep her eyes shut any longer. She opened them fully and got her first good look at the man.

Tall, he was at least a couple of inches over six feet. He had on a muscle shirt that displayed arms as big as her waist with tattoos running from shoulder to wrist. She would not be going hand to hand with him in a fight even if her hands were free. Ellen stayed still and just watched him. Fear threatened to choke her, but she kept her face blank. She hoped. "What do you want?"

He didn't move to enter the room, just stood in the doorway. "All I want is the puppy. You give me the little golden puppy and you're free to go."

Right, like she believed that. She'd seen his face. She knew what it meant. "You want the one with the code embedded in his chip."

His eyes narrowed and his nostrils flared. "Yeah."

"What does it mean?"

"Doesn't matter to you." He checked his phone. "Be ready to go for a ride."

"Where?"

"You'll find out. And if your friend can't follow directions, you're dead."

She swallowed. "What friend?" Surely he didn't mean Lee.

"Dude with the dogs."

He meant Lee. While fear had been right there with her ever since she'd awakened in the room, it hit her full force now. She stood. "What are the directions he's supposed to follow?"

"The ones I gave him. But all you need to worry about is that as long as I get the dog, they get you."

Ellen found no comfort in the words because, while the words sounded good, the look in his eyes said he had no intention of letting her go anywhere. He unlocked the door, stepped outside and then back in. He tossed her a bottle of water and she caught it with hands that were close to numb. "Be back shortly."

"Can you at least loosen the tape? I can't feel my hands."

He laughed. And then he was gone. The soft click of the lock told her the clock was ticking and she needed to figure something out fast. She flexed her fingers around the bottle. As much as she wanted to chug it, she couldn't take a chance it had been drugged. She flung the water bottle on the cot, moved to the wooden chair, picked it up and slammed it against the wall. It shattered into several large pieces. She picked up one of the bigger ones and hefted it. It could work. Maybe.

But first she examined each broken piece for something sharp. *A screw.* It would have to do. She sat on the floor and positioned the piece of wood with the screw sticking out of it between her feet. Then she leaned forward and started scraping the tape over the sharp end of the screw. Sweat ran down her face but she didn't stop, and finally she cut into the tape far enough that a hard yank pulled it apart.

Blood flowed. The pain was sharp enough to make her eyes tear. She took a deep breath, flexed her fingers and massaged her hands. First one, then the other.

Finally, when she felt she could, she grabbed the piece of wood with the screw and took it over to the window. She slid the end of the screw into the shallow crack left between the plywood and the wall. With a grunt, she shoved it hard and heard the squeak of nails as the wood started to separate. She pressed again and the bottom edge popped out. She tossed the piece of chair aside and wedged her fingers underneath.

She started to pull when she heard the lock turn once again.

"I have to go," Lee said. "You heard what he said. I'm to come alone and no cops."

"It's too dangerous," Tristan protested again.

Lee kept his temper under control. Barely. "It's too dangerous for Ellen if I don't show up. He called *me.* He told *me* no cops. If we mess this up, Ellen could die."

"He's planning on killing her anyway," Ryder said quietly. "But as long as he believes we're following his orders, we might be able to get to her before he does it."

Lee flinched at Ryder's words. "Then, someone better come up with a plan that gets her out in one piece because her death is not an option."

"No, it's not," Ryder said. "Lee's right. He needs to be there and he needs a wire. We'll cover him."

Lee nodded. "Fine, get me the wire."

"I've got one in my SUV," Tristan said. He went to get it. When he returned, Ryder went to work, getting Lee wired up and checking to make sure everything was working. He clapped Lee on the shoulder. "We're good to go."

Chief Jones leaned against his vehicle and watched the action. He had a sad, resigned look on his face. When he caught Lee watching, his features hardened and he cleared his throat.

"Could you get a location on her phone?" Tristan asked the chief.

Chief Jones hitched his belt. "No."

"So she could be anywhere," Lee said. "What if he doesn't have her with him?"

"If he wants the puppy," Ryder said, "he'll have her with him. You're going to hold the puppy and demand that he allow you to see her. Once you see she's alive, we'll take it from there. Is your earpiece working?"

"Yes."

"Then, you'll hear everything I say, and I'll be able to hear you. Don't take matters into your own hands, understand?"

"Yes."

"Send me the address."

Lee did.

Tristan looked up. "I've got it programmed in. According to my information, it's an abandoned house on the outskirts of town. Used to belong to the Colson fam-

ily, longtime residents of Desert Valley, but it was fore-
closed on when the senior Mr. Colson died a year and a
half ago. His children never made a single payment on
the house and the bank repossessed it."

"Let me guess, the same bank that got robbed," Lee
said.

"Yes." Lee waited while the man studied the information in front of him. "But the house was never sold and
has been sitting empty for the past few months. They
must have found it and moved in while they planned how
to get a hold of the dogs." He shook his head. "There's
no way to sneak up on this guy. Not in vehicles. He'll
see us coming a mile away. Literally."

Shane pointed to the lake that abutted the backyard.
"We can come in this way. In a boat."

"Where are you going to get a boat at this short notice?" Lee asked.

"Someone who lives on the lake will have one somewhere," Ryder said. "We'll simply borrow one for this,
then put it back when we're done."

"And if they don't?"

Ryder rubbed a hand over his jaw. "We'll figure something out. If worse comes to worse, we can swim across."

"But the front," Tristan said. "We've got to approach
from the front and he's going to be watching."

Lee drew in a deep breath. "Then, I've got to go in
alone."

"No way," Shane said. He motioned to Tristan to move
closer. "Let me see the property layout."

Shane, Tristan and Ryder crowded around the tab-
let. Lee watched them mutter and listened to them plan.
Never had he prayed harder in his life.

The chief blew out a sigh. "All right. We don't have

any more time to discuss this. We'll get the puppy from Sophie and get this wrapped up."

"Let's move folks."

Lee took the passenger seat of Ryder's SUV while Ryder helped his dog, Titus, into the backseat, then slipped behind the wheel.

Ellen stared at the man who'd opened the door. The gun in his left hand was steady—and trained on her chest. She gripped the piece of wood, ready to use it as a weapon. "Freddie?"

He jerked. "You remember me?"

"Of course. How did you get mixed up in this mess?"

"You meet all kinds of interesting people in prison." He licked his lips and glanced over his shoulder. She almost made a move, but he looked back to her too quickly. If she could distract him…

"Where's your partner?" she asked. "The big guy?"

"Taking care of stuff."

His shifty eyes and nervous shuffling had her on high alert. "What is it?"

He licked his lips again. "I want it all for myself and you're going to help me get it."

"Are you using, Freddie?"

"Doesn't matter. Now tell me what was on that dog's chip."

"Why?"

"Because it will tell me where the money is."

"What money?"

"From the bank," he snarled. "I had a cell mate who told me all about his big haul and how he was going to be living it up when he got out."

"And who is this cell mate? Where is he?"

"Dead." Freddie glanced over his shoulder and back again so quickly she had no chance to move. "He'll be back soon."

"Who is he?"

"My cell mate's brother, Trevor."

Ellen's mind was clearing fast. He was talking about the bank robbery in Flagstaff from six months ago. The big guy who'd kidnapped her was the brother of Freddie's cell mate. A cell mate who was now dead. And that cell mate had been involved in the bank robbery. "Where did he go?"

"To get everything set up." He shoved the gun at her and she flinched. Ducked. "So while he's occupied, tell me where the dog is now."

"And if I tell you, what do I get?"

"I don't shoot you."

She shivered. "You can't shoot me, Freddie. Trevor needs me. He's going to exchange me for the puppy. If you shoot me, he's going to be very unhappy with you."

"Won't matter if I'm not around for him to kill. Now—" he jabbed the gun at her again "—where is the dog?"

"Hidden away," she said softly. "We knew you were after him, so we hid him."

"I know that! Where?"

He took a step closer and she swung the piece of wood like a baseball bat, catching him across the arm. He screamed, and the gun fell from his fingers and skidded across the concrete floor. She brought her palm up and caught him in the jaw with the heel of her hand. His head snapped back and he let out another cry. A final kick in the stomach had him doubling over. She had no time to retrieve the weapon.

She bolted from the room and slammed the door. Before she could turn the key that was still in the lock, he had it open. She turned to run. Felt his fingers twist in the back of her shirt. He slammed her against the wall and her head snapped back. Pain raced up her neck and into the base of her skull, but she couldn't stop now. She kicked out and caught him in the knee.

He cried out, and dropped to the ground.

A gunshot sent her diving beside him. Freddie screamed again and then again as another shot sounded. Ellen froze, waiting for the pain to kick in, but when nothing happened, she opened her eyes and found herself staring into Freddie's dead, vacant eyes. "No," she whispered.

She rolled to her feet and spun toward the exit.

Something hard pressed against the back her head. "Ah!" More pain raced through the lower part of her skull.

"Move and you'll die," the man behind her growled.

She froze.

"Good girl. Now walk."

EIGHTEEN

Tristan pulled to a stop just at the edge of the property out of sight of the house. The van behind them did the same. The land stretched out, and Lee knew it went all the way up to the front door of the house. A house that sat in a shallow valley on the edge of a lake that might be a point of entrance for them. Trees dotted the yard. "A good place to hide someone you kidnapped," Lee muttered.

"Yes." Tristan left the van running. Dash yapped in the back in his carrier.

Lee slipped out of the vehicle and around to the driver's side. Tristan vacated the driver's seat and Lee took it over.

"Now remember," Tristan said, "keep him talking. I'm just going to get situated, then you can go."

"He's probably going to check the vehicle. You think he won't know about stow-'n'-go?"

"He might know about it, but hopefully he won't think about it. It's a chance we have to take. I can't let you go in there without protection. This van's been altered to fit an officer under the floorboard. I can get out and get a shot at him as long as you can keep him distracted."

Lee grunted. "I'll keep him distracted, all right." He glanced in the back at the dogs. "Are you going to let them out?"

"No, he'll just shoot at them. We'll keep them in here for the time being."

Lee waited until Tristan was hidden by the removable panel in the back then put the van in Drive and stepped on the gas pedal. His heart thudded as he rolled slowly toward the house. Finally it came into view. The house was a two-story Victorian and needed a good coat of paint. It had an attached two-car garage with another garage set apart from the main house.

Had he hurt her? Would she be all right? Of course she would. *Right, God? Please, God, let her be all right.*

Lee stopped about three-quarters of the way up the long drive. A gray van sat parked off to the side, backed up to the edge of the house.

The front door opened and Ellen stepped out onto the porch. A man followed right behind her. The same man who'd come to the center in a wheelchair. The same man who now had a gun pressed to the back of her head. "Ellen!"

She blanched when she saw him. "Lee! What are you doing here?"

"Trading a puppy for you."

Trevor pushed Ellen in front of him, his eyes never landing in one spot for very long. "You came alone?"

"That's what you said to do."

The man's gaze roamed again. Apparently he liked what he saw. "Bring the dog up here."

Tristan's voice came through the earpiece loud and clear. "He's not going to check the van. I'm not sure I like that. Something happened but we don't have time to figure out what. Ask him where Freddie is."

"Where's Freddie?" Lee asked.

Trevor froze. "Freddie's got you covered, so if you try anything, he'll blow you away."

"There's no one out here, Lee," Tristan said. "We checked."

"Freddie's dead, Lee! He killed him!" Ellen's voice sounded breathless. Trevor gave her a violent shake and she cried out.

Lee started forward, his only thought to get Ellen away from the man hurting her.

"Come any closer and she dies, Mr. Hero."

Lee froze.

"Distract him. Tell him to let Ellen go first."

Lee shifted the puppy's crate to his other hand. "I have the puppy. Let her go."

"I want to see the dog! Now!" He jammed the gun tighter against Ellen's head.

She flinched but never took her eyes from Lee. He tried to reassure her with just a look. Her gaze darted to the van. He gave a slight nod. Her eyes narrowed and he could almost see her brain spinning as she tried to formulate a plan.

Lee set the crate on the ground and opened the cage. He pulled a leash from it and then snapped it to Dash's collar. The puppy walked out of his portable home and started sniffing the ground around him. Lee looked back at Ellen and the man who held her. "Now let her go."

"Walk him up here and give him to her. Hand her the leash."

Lee hesitated.

"Do it!"

"Go ahead, Lee," Tristan said. "I've got you covered. Shane and James are coming up the back now that we've got Little's attention focused on us out here. They came across the lake in a small boat and are now on land in the backyard."

Lee stepped forward and Dash trotted at his side like a good puppy. Like Lee had taught him to do. He kept his eyes on Ellen. She looked beyond him and he knew she was looking for backup.

Lee continued to approach. He passed the leash to Ellen, who took it without looking away from him. He could see her mind whirling, searching for escape, for the right move that would release her but wouldn't get her killed. It was all he could do not to grab the gun from the back of her head or try to land a punch that would allow her to run. But he couldn't take that chance.

"Now back up and get in your van."

Lee didn't budge. "I'm not going anywhere until you release her."

"You can get back in your van or I can put a bullet in her head then yours. Now move!"

Lee locked eyes with Ellen. Fury and fear smoldered there. He backed up as ordered.

"Keep going, Lee," Tristan said.

Lee continued his backward walk until his back was against the front fender of the van. "What now?" he called.

"Now we get in my van and drive away—I'll release her when I'm sure I'm not being followed."

Lee took a step forward only to stop when Little pushed Ellen ahead of him, down the steps and toward the gray van. He had to do something. "Not yet, Lee," Tristan said. "Just hold on."

* * *

Ellen wasn't quite sure who was where, but she knew no one would have let Lee come out here alone. Assuming he told anyone where he was going. Yet she had a feeling there was someone in the van with him—she just wasn't sure who. She'd flipped through escape scenario after escape scenario and hadn't thought of one that wound up with her not being shot. And now Lee was part of the equation.

She let Trevor push her toward the gray van but had no intention of letting him get her inside. Because once she was in, she was dead. She held the leash and the puppy, who happily walked along beside her while the muzzle of the gun never left the back of her head.

They stopped at the van. "Pick him up and put him in," Trevor ordered.

"I'm going to have to bend down to do that," she said.

"Bend down. My bullet will reach that far."

Her heart thudded as she bent. His gun followed her. One twitch of his finger and she would be dead. The fact didn't do a whole lot for her nerves, but an idea hit her. She unclipped the leash from the dog's collar and slapped his hind end with the metal end. He gave a startled yelp and darted under the van.

Trevor shouted a curse. "Get him!"

And for a brief second, the gun was gone from the back of her head. She dived to the ground and rolled, kicking out. She caught his wrist and the pistol flew from his hand. She scrambled to get away from him, but fingers clamped down around her left ankle. A shot rang out and Trevor gave a scream, but didn't release his hold. She kicked again, but had no leverage.

"Ellen!"

Another shot hit the dirt next to him. He jerked her toward him and she saw his fist coming toward her. Ellen threw her arm up to block it. The pain lanced through her and she knew she had to get away from him.

Then he was off her. She rolled to see Lee and Trevor exchanging blows. She launched herself to her feet and flinched when Trevor caught Lee with a harsh jab to his left cheek. The skin split and blood streamed, but Lee didn't stop. He came back around with a hard elbow to Trevor's chin. The man spun and went down, and Ellen threw herself onto his back, a knee to his spine. The air whooshed from his lungs and then they were surrounded by law enforcement. "Police! Don't move! Don't move!"

Ellen held a hand up. Tristan slapped his cuffs into her palm, and she snapped them around the still-breathless criminal. Then pushed off his back to land on the ground with a thud. She let out a breath then found herself enveloped in a crushing embrace.

She breathed in. Lee. "Ellen, are you okay?"

"Yeah. Yes, I'm fine. Major headache, but that means I'm alive if I can feel pain. I'm all right with that. Are you okay?"

"Yes, but I wasn't kidnapped and held prisoner for the past few hours." He pulled her out of the way while Tristan, Shane and the others hauled Trevor to his feet. Blood flowed from the wound in his shoulder. Lee followed her gaze. "Looks like he'll live."

"That's more than can be said for poor Freddie."

"You said Trevor shot him."

"He did," Ellen said.

Chief Jones had been listening in and moved toward the house. "He's not in there," Ellen said. "He's in that separate garage."

The chief nodded. "Are you sure you're all right? He didn't hurt you?"

"Like someone once told me, I've got a pretty hard head. I'll be fine."

He gave a relieved smile. "Good." He headed for the garage she indicated and motioned for Deputy Donaldson to follow him.

Louise touched Ellen on the arm as she passed. "I'm glad you're all right."

"Thanks.

"Sure."

She watched them go, then turned back to Lee. Everyone else was busy with the crime scene. They seemed to have forgotten she and Lee were there. He led her back to the van out of sight of the others and leaned down and kissed her. Ellen froze for only a second before she kissed him back, putting all of the emotion she'd had to hold in check over the past few hours into the kiss. In turn, she felt his fear come through, fear he'd never see her again, never hold her again. When he lifted his head, the sheen of tears in his eyes mirrored hers. "I love you, Ellen," he whispered.

And she couldn't hold back the tears any longer. "I love you, too, Lee. I always have. I never stopped. I'm so sorry about everything."

He swiped the tears from her cheeks with his thumb. "I don't know what it will take to make sure we live happily ever after, but I'm telling you right now, we're going to figure it out. Okay?"

She choked on a teary laugh and nodded. "Okay."

He pulled her back to his chest and kissed her head. "I know your mother doesn't like me, but maybe I can win her over."

"I think she just doesn't know you," Ellen said. "Once she hears how you helped save my life, she'll be forever grateful."

He dropped to one knee and held her hand. "I don't have a ring yet. I'm not very good with fancy words, but I almost lost you today and I'm not waiting another second."

Ellen's heart thudded, nearly popping from her chest. "Lee," she whispered. "What are you—?"

"Ellen, this isn't the time or the place or how I thought about doing this, but after what we just went through, I'm not waiting a second longer. I want to marry you. I love you. I've loved you since high school. Will you do me the honor of becoming my wife?"

She dropped to her knees in front of him and cupped his face. "You're sure?"

"Never more sure of anything in my life."

The look in his eyes convinced her. "Then, yes, I'll marry you. Tomorrow if you want."

He kissed her. Hard and swift and full of leashed passion. Then he trailed little kisses over her eyes and nose, cheeks and chin. The smile on his face was brilliant. She knew hers rivaled his.

"So are you guys getting married?"

Ellen jerked and turned to see Shane, Tristan, James, David and the chief watching them with silly grins on their faces. She looked back at Lee. "We sure are."

NINETEEN

Two days later

Lee held the door while Ellen stepped inside her mother's hospital room. She walked to the woman's side and reached for her hand. "Sure wish you would wake up, Mom," she said softly.

Lee took note of the machines and wires and the fact that Marian looked as though she'd aged twenty years. All the anger he'd harbored toward her over the past years fell away. He walked over to Ellen's side and put an arm around her shoulders. She leaned into him and sighed. "We won't stop praying for her," he said.

"I know. Thank you for forgiving her." She turned and slipped her arms around his waist. He'd never tire of her doing that. He held her, relishing the feel of her finally where he'd wanted her to be for so long. "And we won't give up on finding Veronica's killer."

He kissed the top of her head. "Yeah. I know." He sighed and just enjoyed having her in his arms. "How's your head?"

"Better."

"Nightmares?"

"A few. But mostly about losing you."

He squeezed her closer. "Never."

"And what about you? Do you have nightmares, too?"

He ran a hand through her hair and tilted her chin so he could look into her eyes. "Only about losing you."

Tears swam to the surface and she blinked. Her arms tightened around him. "Never," she whispered.

The door opened and the doctor entered. He nodded. "Hi there."

Ellen slipped from Lee's arms and acknowledged the man with a smile. "Hi."

"She's still being stubborn about waking up, isn't she?" he asked. He walked over to check the machines.

"Well, stubborn has her still alive, so..." Ellen shrugged. "She'll wake up when she's ready." Maybe if she kept repeating that, she'd believe it.

The doctor nodded. "Yes. I think she might actually be doing a bit better. She's not awake, but she's responding to some stimuli when we touch her feet."

"Really?" Hope shone in her eyes and she moved to her mother. She leaned down and kissed her cheek. "Wake up, Mom. I want to talk to you."

Lee stepped up beside her. "Wake up, Marian. We've got a lot to discuss. Like the fact that Ellen let me drive your Jeep."

Ellen choked on a laugh and lightly punched his arm. "Lee!"

"Well, you did."

"Yes, but you weren't supposed to tell her."

"If it gets her to wake up, then it's worth it."

Ellen's gaze softened. "Yes, yes it is. Wake up so you can yell at me about it, okay, Mom?"

There was no response, but Ellen couldn't help but let herself believe that her mom had heard her.

"Are you ready to go?" Lee asked softly.

"Sure."

The doctor lifted a hand in goodbye and Lee held the door for her. She slipped out of the room and into the hall. Lee stayed right by her side. "Want to get Carly and Dash and go for a hike?"

"Sure, that sounds great."

They left together and headed for the assistance center to pick up Dash. Once there, they found work going on. Gabby and her mother were working with Popcorn, who was responding beautifully to the little girl's commands. After a hug, Ellen exchanged a few words with the other employees while Lee went to get Dash.

The puppy spun in circles of excitement when he saw him, and Lee knew he'd have a hard time putting the animal in someone else's hands. But he would do it. Because that was the way it was supposed to be.

He snapped the leash on the dog's collar and walked back into the lobby to find Ellen speaking with Tristan.

"I think a puppy would be great for her."

"For who?" Lee asked.

"Tristan's sister."

"She's having a hard time right now," Tristan said.

"I'm sorry. That's tough."

"Yeah." He tapped his chin, a thoughtful look on his face. "So I think I'll go by the county shelter and take a look around."

"Take your sister with you," Lee said. "Let her pick the one she wants."

Tristan nodded. "Good idea. The only problem is, I may wind up with more than one if I do it that way."

Lee laughed and Ellen smiled. Tristan sighed. "All right. I guess I'll get out of here. I've still got work to do on Veronica's case."

Lee sobered and shook the man's hand. "Thanks for all you're doing." He glanced at Ellen. "I've had my eyes opened to the fact you're all doing more than I thought you were."

"Of course. I know it's hard. Sometimes it's a slow process."

"I've come to realize that."

"Ellen said you were heading back to finish vet school."

"Someday soon, I hope."

"You'll be a good one."

"So what was the code on the chip on Dash?" Ellen asked. "It's been so crazy, I haven't had a chance to even find out."

"Lee figured it out," Tristan said. "It was latitude and longitude for where the money from the bank robbery was buried."

"No way," Ellen said. "Someone actually buried the money?"

"Yeah. Lee told us to try the coordinates and there it was. Easy peasy."

She looked at Lee. "Impressive."

He felt the heat in his neck and gave a shrug. "I was working with some kids at the training center and the map on the wall gave me the idea. I didn't know for sure, but turns out it was a good guess."

"Exactly. So," Tristan said, "that's one case closed. Now to find out who stole the evidence from the police station, find Marco, the missing puppy, and get Veronica's case shut. See you guys later."

Tristan left. Ellen scratched Carly's ears. Dash jumped at her and Carly nudged him away. The puppy came back for more and soon it was a game between the two.

Ellen laughed at the two animals and looked around her. She was blessed. Her gaze landed on Lee. Super blessed. Why had she fought it so hard? Being kidnapped and almost killed had certainly put her into a different kind of mind-set.

Life was short and it was precious. It was time to spend it with those she loved. Including Lee. True, Veronica's murderer was still out there, but she had a feeling it wouldn't be too much longer until the person was found. Each day they seemed to get closer.

Lee pulled her close for a quick kiss and her heart tripped over itself in joy. She smiled up at him. "I could get used to that."

"Me, too. When do you want to get married?"

Her eyes widened. "Um. I don't know."

"You haven't even thought about it?" He looked slightly wounded.

Ellen slapped his shoulder with a light punch. He caught her hand and kissed her fingers. She sighed. "Of course I've thought about it. I've thought of little else. And I can't decide."

He sobered. "We can wait until your mother wakes up on one condition."

"What's that?"

"That you don't change your mind."

She kissed him long and hard. When she pulled back, she looked into his dark eyes. "I'm not changing my mind. Get that through your head."

"Okay."

"Okay?"

"Yep. You've convinced me. We can wait until she wakes up."

Ellen bit her lip. "I don't think that's necessary, but I love you for offering."

He kissed her again. "And I love you."

"You realize I might be assigned out of town once the murders are solved."

"I know. It's okay. Once you find out your assignment, if I have to change schools to go with you, I will. Or whatever. We'll figure it out." He tapped her nose. "So when?"

"Soon."

"That's good enough for me. Ready?"

"Ready."

His fingers closed around hers and, with the dogs at their heels, they walked out of the center together.

She'd come to love that word. *Together.*

Forever was her next favorite.

Forever together.

* * * * *

If you liked this ROOKIE K-9 UNIT *novel,*
watch for the next book in the series,
SECRETS AND LIES by Shirlee McCoy.

Dear Reader,

I appreciate you so much! Without you, I wouldn't be able to do a job I adore. Thank you for reading! I hope you've enjoyed Ellen and Lee's story and the rest of the continuity books in this series. Lee had to overcome quite a lot. Wrongly imprisoned for a crime he didn't commit, set up by someone who was supposed to protect him, he could have chosen the path of bitterness. Instead, he chose to move on with his life, to make something of himself in spite of the curveball life threw at him. I admire him for that.

Sometimes when things don't go my way or I feel like I've been wronged, I want to get even. But that never solves anything. It takes a real hero to choose the high road, a path that's not always the easiest to find and follow, but one that never leads to regrets. Praying that if you have a situation where you can go one way or the other, you'll choose the right path, the one that will let you come out a hero.

Now go read a good book.

Blessings,

Lynette Eason

COMING NEXT MONTH FROM
Love Inspired® Suspense

Available August 2, 2016

SECRETS AND LIES
Rookie K-9 Unit • by Shirlee McCoy
When someone tries to kill pregnant teacher Ariel Martin at the local high school, her student's brother, K-9 officer Tristan McKeller, saves her. But can he unravel the secrets in the single mother's past and discover who's after her?

SILENT SABOTAGE
First Responders • by Susan Sleeman
Emily Graves moves to a small town to take over her aunt's bed-and-breakfast...and finds her life in jeopardy. Now if she wants to survive—and save the family business—Emily must turn to Deputy Sheriff Archer Reed for protection.

FATAL VENDETTA • by Sharon Dunn
While reporting on a fire, television journalist Elizabeth Kramer is kidnapped. And with the help of her rival, blogger Zachery Beck, she escapes. Now, as Elizabeth's stalker becomes increasingly violent, Zach is determined to keep her safe.

PLAIN COVER-UP • by Alison Stone
Taking a leave from his job, FBI agent Dylan Hunter expects a chance to relax in a small Amish community—until his former love, Christina Jennings, is attacked. Somebody wants her dead...and she needs his help to stay alive.

DEAD END • by Lisa Phillips
Former CIA agent Nina Holmes is determined to find her mother's killer. And when her investigation puts Nina in danger, she and US marshal Wyatt Ames must solve the murder...or Nina could become a serial killer's next victim.

RANCH REFUGE
Rangers Under Fire • by Virginia Vaughan
When former army ranger Colton Blackwell saves Laura Jackson from an attempted kidnapping, he takes her to his ranch for safety. But when the loan shark trying to collect on her father's debt sends attackers from all directions, will Colton's protection be enough?

LOOK FOR THESE AND OTHER LOVE INSPIRED BOOKS WHEREVER BOOKS ARE SOLD, INCLUDING MOST BOOKSTORES, SUPERMARKETS, DISCOUNT STORES AND DRUGSTORES.

LISCNM0716

SPECIAL EXCERPT FROM

Love Inspired
SUSPENSE

*When a pregnant widow becomes the target of a killer,
a rookie K-9 unit officer and his loyal dog must step up
to protect her.*

*Read on for an excerpt from
SECRETS AND LIES,
the next book in the exciting K-9 cop miniseries
ROOKIE K-9 UNIT.*

Glass shattering.

Rookie K-9 officer Tristan McKeller heard it as he
hooked his K-9 partner to a lead. The yellow Lab cocked his
head to the side, growling softly.

"What is it, boy?" Tristan asked, scanning the school
parking lot. Only one other vehicle was parked there—a
shiny black minivan that he knew belonged to Ariel Martin,
the teacher he was supposed be meeting with. He was
late. Of course. That seemed to be the story of his life this
summer. Work was crazy, and his sister was crazier, and
finding time to meet with her summer-school teacher? He'd
already canceled two previous meetings. He couldn't cancel
this one. Not if Mia had any hope of getting through summer
school.

He was going to be even later than he'd anticipated,
though, because Jesse was still growling, alerted to
something that must have to do with the shattering glass.

"Find!" he commanded, and Jesse took off, pulling
against the leash in his haste to get to the corner of the
building and around it. Trained in arson detection, the dog

had an unerring nose for almost anything. Right now, he was on a scent, and Tristan trusted him enough to let him have his head.

Glass glittered on the pavement twenty feet away, and Jesse beelined for it, barking raucously, his tail stiff and high.

A woman appeared in the window. Dark hair. Pale skin. Freckles. Very pregnant belly that wasn't cooperating as she struggled to crawl through the opening. Ariel Martin. The newest teacher at Desert Valley High School. Smart. Enthusiastic. Patient. He'd heard that from more than one parent. He'd even heard it from Mia.

"You okay?" he asked, running to her side.

She shook her head, dark gray eyes wide with shock, a smear of blood on her right hand. She'd cut herself. It looked deep, but she didn't seem to notice. "He's got a gun. He tried to shoot me."

Don't miss SECRETS AND LIES
by Shirlee McCoy, available wherever
Love Inspired® Suspense books and ebooks are sold.

www.LoveInspired.com